"Going in or coming out?"

"Sorry." As Lily jumped aside to free up the doorway, she recognized Nick's superlative smile beaming like the sun, warming every cell in her body. His nose was rosy, and his quizzical eyes shimmered with moisture as if he'd been in the frigid wind for too long. She bit her tongue to prevent any wild thoughts from rushing past her shivering lips.

"Hey, are you following me?" He winked.

"I, um…" His distinctive musk and cinnamon scent derailed her train of thought. She hid her smile while brushing away an escaped curl tickling her chin. Did her best to contain the butterflies fluttering in her belly.

"*Well?*" Nick cocked his head in scrutiny. "I'm cold and hungry. How about you?" He grimaced, underdressed for the blustery weather in a black leather jacket with a red scarf tucked into the collar. "Care to join me?"

Thank you
for reading.
I hope you
enjoy it! xo

Sleeping with Santa

by

Debra Druzy

Debra Druzy

This is a work of fiction. Names, characters, places, and incidents are either the product of the author's imagination or are used fictitiously, and any resemblance to actual persons living or dead, business establishments, events, or locales, is entirely coincidental.

Sleeping with Santa

COPYRIGHT © 2014 by Debra Druzy

Cover Art by *Angela Anderson*

The Wild Rose Press, Inc.
PO Box 708
Adams Basin, NY 14410-0708
Visit us at www.thewildrosepress.com

Publishing History
First Champagne Rose Edition, 2014
Print ISBN 978-1-62830-737-5
Digital ISBN 978-1-62830-738-2

Published in the United States of America

Dedications

Happy Birthday to my little sister,
December-baby,
and favorite redhead—Cindy
Thank you for the inspiration to write this story.
~*~
To KP, KVP, JLP, & TB
Thank you for being…everything to me!
xo~kisses & hugs~ox
~*~
To My Loving, Sweet, Devoted Mother
Thank you for feeding my family so I can write!
And everything else!!
~*~
To Dad
Thank you for believing in me & babysitting!
Can you believe I wrote a book?
~*~
For Grandma Violet, Grandpa Harry,
Grandma Jean, & Grandpa Honey
I miss you every day.
~*~
As Violet always said,
"I don't love you—I'm *crazy* about you!"
~*~
XOXO

Chapter One

Lily Lane stepped into the warmth of Ray's Liquor Store with twenty minutes left to her lunch break, a wad of cash, and a mile-long Christmas list.

Well, not exactly a mile, but it was long enough to require a shopping cart. And the wad was just crumpled singles and fives she'd collected in the tip jar throughout the last two months, specifically for this pathetic shopping spree.

From his perch at the counter, the gray-haired owner peeked over his reading glasses and put down the newspaper. "Let me guess…cheap champagne?"

"Oh, Ray, you know me so well." It wasn't the greatest gift, but it wasn't the worst either. And it was better than giving nothing at all. As her mother used to say, *it's the thought that counts*.

"How much? And how many?"

"Well…" She choked on the bitter taste of pride and winced. "I got two-hundred bucks. And I need…twenty bottles."

At least Ray didn't flinch this year. He offered four cases of six bottles, calling it even. They settled the deal by the stockroom door just as the jingle bell announced another customer's arrival. A *real* customer, no doubt.

"I'll bring the cart back later."

Poised to leave, she spied the person's face—a *new* face...make that a *handsome* new face—and changed direction. She had to be sure he wasn't a mirage or just one of the neighborhood dirt bags all cleaned up.

The trouble with knowing everybody in this godforsaken speck of a suburban town meant knowing everybody's personal business. She didn't want anyone knowing any more of her business than what they probably already knew. In her book, dating local guys was as taboo as dating a fireman.

The stranger followed Ray down the aisle until all she could see was dark hair over the stacked boxes of margarita mixers.

She ducked behind the rack of dusty wine bottles to sneak a peek. *Turn around, turn around. I don't have all day. Turn around already.*

When he stepped into her narrow line of vision, her heart stopped. She clamped her palm over her mouth to stifle the stunned gasp at *Adonis* in a black leather jacket.

Broad shoulders tapered toward a trim waist and lean legs in fitted jeans. Relaxed but not sloppy, neat but not boring. Sculpted cheeks. Strong chin. Dark slashes for eyebrows. His nose had a slight bump at the bridge as if he'd broken it at some point in his gorgeous life. Full, bow-shaped lips made her think of kissing...

One way ticket to Swoon-City, please.

She'd love to get him in the barber chair if only to run her fingers through that thick mane. By the threads of silver sparkling around his temples, he had to be over thirty.

He was *hot*. Totally hot. The total-package kind of hot. The kind of hot that made her want to know what he ate for breakfast so she could serve it to him in bed. If she had a type, he'd be *it*.

His swagger radiated the confidence of an alpha that lured her out of hiding in order to get a better look, and she walked right into his wave of musky cologne.

"You're still here?" Ray asked.

"Something's wrong with the, uh, wheels," she lied with a clear conscience.

"Let me take care of the gentleman first. Then I'll help you move those cases to another shopping cart."

"Take your time. I can wait."

It was impossible not to stare at *the gentleman* at such close range. He looked like a gorgeous grizzly bear. She pretended to study the clever advertisements on the walls. But every time their eyes touched her system screamed: *WE HAVE A WINNER!*—like the bells and blinking lights on the High-Striker hammer game at the carnival.

"That'll be three hundred and fourteen dollars," Ray said.

For two bottles of booze?

Adonis pulled out a fat roll of cash and paid with hundred dollar bills. "One bottle's coming with me. Ship the other to this address." He scribbled on the back of the receipt and handed it to Ray.

Then bedroom eyes wandered toward the contents of Lily's cart and continued to rove up her body. Electricity surged under her skin—a *zing* if she ever felt one.

Every cell in her body vibrated the confirmation: *He. Is. The. One*!

A slow lethal smile spread across his clean-shaven face. "Havin' a party?"

Why—you wanna come? Lily shook her head no. With her heart pinned in her chest, it was impossible to breathe, never mind speak.

"You know what they say, 'When you need a shopping cart in a liquor store you mean business.'" He winked, making her knees wobble.

The wheels rolled from under her weight, and the cart bumped into the wall without damaging the merchandise. "Oh, would you look at that? Must have fixed itself."

"I'll get the door for you," Adonis offered on the way out. His delicious drawl sounded so wonderful, she wanted to hear it whispering in her ear. Late at night. Under the covers.

"Uh, okay." Lily choked on the simple words. She wiped clammy palms on her velour track pants before gripping the handle.

"Where're ya parked? I'll help you load it into the car."

Thank God for the brisk wind to cool her face, flaring with heat. "It's in the lot all the way around back. But that's okay—I work three doors down." She pointed to the red, white, and blue-striped pole. "I'll leave it in the shop until closing time."

He strolled beside her like a happy puppy, swinging his purchase in a brown paper bag, choking the bottle by the neck. His long legs seemed to reach the height of her shoulders, but he kept his stride in time with her slower, shorter steps.

"They sure decorate early around here." He nodded toward the procession of telephone poles being dressed in green garland and scarlet bows.

"A little *too* early."

"Oh, I'm not complaining. *Red's* my favorite color." His voice dropped a sultry octave.

Lily pushed windblown copper curls out of her eyes, wondering what he meant by the remark. Either he was hitting on her or *really* liked Christmas.

Outside the barbershop, Adonis made himself comfortable on the bench reserved for customers, while she stood, squeezing the cart handle like a foam rubber stress ball. Eye to eye, his were so dark she couldn't tell the pupil from the iris. And their lips were in perfect alignment for *kissing*…

"It's real pretty around here." His gaze narrowed on her face.

No doubt, he was referring to the town, but for a moment Lily swore he was talking about her.

"Strange seeing Halloween and Christmas together."

"I know. But that's how we do things in Scenic View. Just can't do one holiday at a time." She looked away in order to break the spell before she lost her balance, considering she already lost her cool, helpless to control her babbling. "We, um, also combine New Year's with Valentine's Day from December twenty-sixth to the weekend after February fifteenth. And if you spend enough time around here you'll realize we celebrate St. Patrick's Day all year—"

Cut off by the clamor of screeching tires and honking horns, their heads snapped in the direction of Mr. Lucky's Pub further down the sidewalk. The hellacious uproar was for some dude staggering across Main Street after an apparent liquid lunch. Thank God no one got hurt.

"Wow. Now, that's some luck of the Irish," Adonis said. "You know a lot about this place."

"I should—I've been living here forever. But not for much longer."

"Oh, yeah." He lifted thick brows. "Where ya going?"

"Closer to the city. Brooklyn. Maybe Queens. I'm not sure. I wish I could live in Manhattan, but it's so expensive. All I want is a cute little apartment and a job in one of those fancy salons. Or maybe a day spa." Gushing to a total stranger felt like free therapy. He nodded as if he were paying attention, even silenced his cell phone ringing inside his jacket, so Lily kept chattering. "It just seems like such a big process."

"Deciding to change who you are into the person you wanna be *is* huge. Some folks never figure it out. At least you know what you want. It'll happen when the time is right."

His profound words resonated with everything she'd been feeling for so long. She wanted to reach out and touch him to be sure he was real, because right now he seemed too good to be true. It'd been so long since she discussed anything on a personal level, communicating beyond the barber chair felt like a lost art.

"I just put my house on the market. You wanna buy it? Just kidding—it's a burden more than anything else. Needs a lot of work. A handyman's nightmare." Lily forced a laugh. "What brings you to Scenic View?"

"My uncle left me some property—a little bungalow on the beach—so I came to check things out. It seems like a nice town if I decide to stay. Maybe. I dunno yet. By the way, I'm Nick."

Caught off-guard by his interjected introduction, she nearly forgot her name. "I, um…I'm Lily."

In the perfunctory code of politeness, he offered his palm in a handshake. "Nice to meet you, Lily." Her name rolled off his tongue like an incantation.

Mesmerized, she took his hand. The firm strength of his long, thick fingers wrapped around hers, transferring his energy up her arm, warming the right side of her body. There it was again—*zing!* She held on longer than the usual greeting only because it felt so good. *Safe. Warm. Connected.* Before he wrenched his arm away, she let her grip go limp, leaving her hand naked without his touch.

"Lily!" Bob's Italian accent invaded her bliss as he leaned his torso out the door, aiming scissors at her. "Whaddaya doin' out here?"

Wishing for a few more moments in heaven with Nick. "Be right there, Bob."

Her boss jutted his chin in their direction. "Who's your friend?"

"This is, um, Nick."

"Say goodbye and get back to work." Bob disappeared inside.

"Well, thanks for the talk." With a quick, tight-lipped smile, she wheeled the cart toward the door, afraid if she opened her mouth she'd say something stupid, like rattle off her phone number—or worse, ask for his.

"Uh-oh. You're not in trouble, are you?"

"No. Bob's all bark. It's his wife whose bite you have to watch."

"Good to know." He nodded, seeming to take it all in. "What time do you close?"

"Why?" Her fingers itched with excitement. "Looking for a trim?"

He raked a hand through dark, wavy layers. "Well, I just had my annual grooming about two weeks ago."

"*Annual grooming*?" She chuckled.

"Here, I'll show you." He dug his wallet from his back pocket and flashed his driver's license.

"Whoa," she said at his marvelous mug shot. But more than his shoulder length rock star locks, what caught her attention was his birthdate. Her dizzy brain couldn't do the math on the spot, but she estimated he was a decade older.

"Do I need an appointment?" He opened the door.

"It's a barbershop." Lily pointed to the sign in the window: *NO APPOINTMENT NECESSARY—WALK-INS WELCOME*.

"Lily!" Bob barked from his workstation. "Shut the door!"

"I gotta go."

Nick lingered as if waiting for something more, then turned and strolled away.

She watched him go, hoping he'd run back to her like in the movies. Only this wasn't a movie, and he was already gone, lost in the crowd.

Hours passed.

Lily was losing hope that he'd return.

It was crazy to think she met her Mr. Right, finally, after all these years, right here in town. In the liquor store no less. What a stupid idea. He probably forgot about her already.

She sat in her empty chair, overhearing Bob and his customer talk about something about someone in a fire department somewhere. Long story short, a firefighter made the ultimate sacrifice battling a raging blaze over the weekend.

Geez. The tragic news was a cruel reminder that life is too short, too fragile. It solidified her mother's golden rule—*never, under any circumstances, fall for a firefighter.*

To avoid the rest of the gruesome details, she hid in the backroom, where she found a laundry basket of clean white towels to fold. But still the inescapable thoughts followed, flooding her mind. *Was he a father? A husband?*

Familiar with the aftershock of such a devastating loss, she closed her eyes and whispered a string of prayers.

Lily hardly remembered a thing about her father's death. But she'd never forget how hard the years that followed were for her mother. The woman lost her husband and her mind all at once.

Scattered memories squeezed the air from her lungs like a vise. Good thing she was already sitting, hanging her head between her knees before the lightheadedness overwhelmed her and the bosses found her passed out. She waited for the sick feeling to pass, but it never would. Not really...Not completely...

"Lily! Customer for you." All the way to the backroom, from behind the cash register, Sophia's shrill voice chased away the ghosts—for now.

"Be right there." She blinked back tears before they could fall.

An eager little boy rushed to Lily's chair, and she tried not to let her disappointment show.

"Santa's coming! Santa's coming!" he squealed. "I saw his mailbox on the sidewalk. You better hurry up and send him your letter so he gets it in time. I can't believe Santa's almost gonna be here!"

Despite being two months early for Christmas, she played along. "Wow, I can hardly believe it! I better write a letter quick."

Once she finished cutting junior's honey-brown mop-top, she jotted the requirements for her farfetched Christmas fantasy on the back of a blank slip from the receipt book. It seemed pointless, but she spelled it out anyway. Her same request for the past few years—a tall order for an *emotionally available* man, something Santa could never deliver.

This year, though, she dared to get specific and scribbled Nick's name just in case miracles do come true.

Until someone made a reasonable offer to buy her rickety old bungalow, she needed another way to supplement her salary. She wasn't keen on living with a stranger but... Out of pure desperation, she flipped to another blank sheet and wrote a *Room-For-Rent/Roommate-Wanted* advertisement.

Before heading home, she returned the shopping cart to Ray's, then power-walked to the firehouse to tack her ad on the community bulletin board.

Circling back to get her car, she passed the red mailbox and dropped her little folded Christmas list in the slot with some big wishful thinking.

Chapter Two

"Where the hell have ya been?" Squinting through the haze of cigar smoke, the chief of the Scenic View Fire Department sat behind his big wooden desk. He checked his wristwatch then pointed to the calendar on the wall. "You know you're a late, dontcha?"

Belated was better than reneging to come at all.

Nick set the big bottle of scotch on the desk. A thank you gift for the position and an apology for being two weeks behind schedule, all wrapped in a brown paper bag.

"I meant to check in sooner, but I've been kinda busy taking care of some personal stuff."

"Have a seat, Captain Knight."

"Call me Nick."

"You got it." The man needed no introduction with the shiny silver nameplate on the door: *Chief William Maresca.* "Sounds like *Fresca*, you know, the soda." Wafting one hand to break up the sweet-smelling smolder curling in the air, he lifted the window with the other, the movement making the buttons on his white collared shirt strain against his protruding belly. "Want a cigar?"

"No, thanks." Nick pulled out a stick of gum from his jacket pocket, folded it into his mouth, and rolled the thin paper between his restless fingers.

"I spoke to your chief in Star Harbor, and we set up this arrangement because it was mutually beneficial. This department is short-staffed. And you need a *change of scenery*—whatever the hell that's supposed to mean." Maresca sat back, making the chair squeak beneath his weight. "Mind filling me in?"

Nick tried keeping it short.

But it was hard to keep it sweet.

Basically, the Star Harbor Fire Chief forced the issue of the transfer. Special assignment. Temporary relocation. However the hell headquarters wanted to file it. The town closed one of the sub-stations. *His* sub-station. They could've transferred anyone. But everyone else had roots. Wives. Kids. Mortgages.

Nick had nothing. Just himself.

And a crazy ex-wife who was taking a permanent vacation in his neighborhood.

The pretext of it all was Nick could use a change of scenery to escape his early mid-life funk. Might as well ship him some place he'd like so he'd never want to return to Star Harbor.

"The only reason I came to Scenic View is because my chief made me. He found a bunch of letters sent to the firehouse addressed to me from an attorney here in town." Nick pulled out an envelope and flashed Maresca the label on the flap. "Being how I don't have any business around here, I just chucked the letters every month without even opening them, figuring it was junk mail. His secretary thought they were thrown away by accident, so she picked them out of the trash and gave them to the chief. The day he dropped the bomb about the transfer, he pulled out a wad of envelopes. Opened one of them. Read it. Showed it to me. I thought it's gotta be a joke. He figured it's worth looking into."

Maresca leaned on his elbows, inching closer with Nick's every word. "Ya killing me with the suspense."

Hesitant to admit his wondrous windfall aloud, like saying the words would be a gigantic jinx, he slid the paper out of the envelope and handed it to Maresca.

"Well, I'm not being sued like I figured. And no one's looking for child support."

"Ah-ha." Maresca scanned the paper and nodded. "I should have put two-and-two together by the last name. You're the one the town's been looking for. Your uncle was a good man. If you don't mind the pun, we considered him a regular *knight in shining armor* around here. He passed away a few years ago. You're just coming around now to claim the estate?"

"Great uncle," Nick said. "I never met him. Guess it took the lawyer some time to track me down. Glad to know the old man was a nice guy."

"A regular saint. When the church burnt down, he paid for everything—from the building to the new Bibles. He was responsible for the community clubhouse. The upgraded playground in Rocketship Park. The expansion to the hospital. Even founded the Secret Santa Society we operate outta the firehouse. *Helluva* guy he was. God rest his soul."

No saint himself, Nick wasn't ready to accept

the honorable challenge of filling the dead man's shoes, although accepting the money had been pretty painless so far.

Maresca handed back the letter, and Nick folded it carefully, putting it away like it was something sacred. It was, after all, the million-dollar letter.

And if it weren't for the Star Harbor Fire Chief forcing him to read it, he never would have known about his great, big, fat inheritance. He hoped the bottle in transit was enough of a thank you until he could do something more, like pay off the guy's mortgage. Or the grandkids' college careers. Something major like that.

With ten million in liquid cash, plus numerous real estate assets dotting Long Island, Nick went from getting by, to being able to buy anything. His first major purchase was a special order custom camper so he could cruise through his impending mid-life crisis in style. He was still a few years away from forty, but when it hit, he'd be ready.

"Well...I guess that's it then?" Maresca sighed.

"What's it?"

"You're here to tell me you're retiring now, aren't you?"

Caught off guard, lost in a daydream, he half-nodded, half-shook his head, and shrugged in an awkward motion. "Wait—what?" *Old guys retire. I'm old...but not that old.* "I'm not retiring."

"Well, that's good, 'cause I need the help. Two guys are out on paternity leave 'til the new year. Headquarters is a little slow processing your paperwork, so you're on limited duty for now. There's plenty to do in-house. We're a municipal department. Things are quiet for the most part. I need someone to handle the Training Officer slot and the Fire Marshal's office. And we have Fire Prevention Day coming up…"

Nick was familiar with it all. "I can do that."

"And the town can always use a few extra hands when it snows. The department helps whenever we can. Independent contractors get paid pretty good for plowing, not that you need the money."

"No problem. I've got a plow for my pickup. Is that all?"

"Well, there is *something* else." Maresca pulled up the vertical window shade. "See the red mailbox across the street?"

Next to the standard blue *USPS* box stood a twin painted red with white lettering—*NORTH POLE.* He'd spotted it yesterday on his way to the liquor store where he met that cute little redhead.

Lily.

He and his libido had a hard time resisting the rarity of a sexy Pippi Longstocking. Too bad she looked about half his age, with the creamy complexion and youthful spray of faint freckles. Her skin lacked the fine lines he noticed creeping into his daily reflection.

How young could she be if she was old enough to buy booze?

Still, he didn't dare go back to see her at the barbershop. Not after her boss waved his pointy shears in his direction.

"If you'll collect the letters, I'll sort them out. I like to read them first before giving them to the Ladies Auxiliary. They give them back to the parents. Or if it's too big of a request—like medical issues or families in crisis—the *Secret Santa Society* gets involved. We've installed wheelchair ramps for the elderly. Bought computers for kids. Paid the electric bill for out-of-work residents. That kind of stuff."

Nick nodded. "Sounds like a good system."

"It was your uncle's idea."

"Well, count me in on the Secret Santa stuff. Besides money, I'm pretty handy, I can donate my time."

"Speaking of your time…" Maresca wavered, and Nick sensed the anvil coming. "I was hoping— since you're new around here, and none of the kids know your face—you might be interested in playing Santa for them at the Christmas party."

Wham! There it was. If he agreed to play Santa, he'd probably get suckered in being the Easter Bunny, too. He fumbled for a viable reason to say no.

"I'd do it myself," Maresca explained, "but I had a knee replacement last year, and I'm still working out the kinks. I can't handle all those kids."

Yeah, good excuse. Feeling the guilt mounting, Nick gave a silent sigh, and said, "Yes," without flinching.

"Good. Now that we got Santa squared away, you have a CPR class to give."

"Now?"

Maresca checked his watch. "In about twenty minutes. I was gonna do it, but since you're here…" He tore off a yellow page from the legal pad with *To-Dos* scribbled during their conversation and handed it to Nick as he limped around the desk. "Come on, I'll give you the grand tour to the basement."

Compared to the modern Star Harbor firehouse, Scenic View's was a relic. Faded red brick on the outside with dark wood and brass trim on the main floor inside showed its age but looked well maintained. Memorabilia from yesteryear adorned the walls. Pale photographs and shiny plaques with names of past officers glinted in two lines along the narrow hallway.

They rode the creaky elevator down one level because Maresca's knees couldn't handle the stairs.

"Where ya staying while you're in town?"

"My uncle's bungalow. Thinking of making some renovations in the spring." *If it doesn't collapse first.*

"Geez." Maresca recoiled. "Don't tell me you're living in that abandoned shack on the beach, way down from the boardwalk."

"I was. But the attorney just told me this morning the town condemned it for fungal mold. And the electrical system wasn't up to code. Is there a decent motel around here?"

"You can try the Hideaway Hotel. They rent rooms by the hour if you catch my drift. Then there's the Scenic View Inn overlooking the marina. That'll run you three bills a night. Or you can check the community bulletin board."

Tacked to the wall was an array of handwritten and professionally printed signs. Nick scanned them all. Car for sale. Babysitter wanted. Dog walker. Dog sitter. House cleaner. House sitter. Landscaper. Room for rent/Roommate wanted.

"Perfect." Maresca plucked the last one and handed it to Nick. "Someone's looking for you."

"I don't think that'll work for me."

"Hang on to it. You never know. Maybe you'll change your mind. In the meantime, stay in the bunkroom as long as you want."

Maresca pushed open a steel door labeled *Training*—by virtue of a piece of silver duct tape printed with black marker—and flipped on a wall switch. "The supply closet is back here."

The room was a blank space, except for the perimeter of folding chairs set up like a horseshoe against pale paneled walls facing a movie screen and a plain metal desk in the corner.

"Everything you need's in here." Maresca led them to another door within the training room and flicked another wall switch, turning on the overhead fluorescent bulbs inside a storage closet bigger than Nick's tiny bungalow.

"Heads up!" Maresca called, and Nick turned in time to catch the soft packages. A pale blue button-down shirt, navy blue standard-issue pants, and a one-size-fits-most clip-on tie. "We're pillars of the community. Gotta look the part."

Nick made a quick change in the locker room before schlepping cumbersome plastic torsos from the closet, setting them in neat rows on the industrial-carpeted floor.

"Here they come." Maresca stepped in the hallway at the sound of footsteps clattering down the metal staircase.

Nick couldn't avoid eavesdropping on the chief having a helluva time coaxing an unwilling female into the room.

"But I took the class last year." Her gentle protest bordered on whining. "Why do I have to sit through it again?"

"They changed the guidelines," Maresca said. "Plus, you're gonna need training on how to use the AED machine. Just get in there, Lily."

Lily! The redheaded girl with the shopping cart in the liquor store—that Lily?

Nick backed into the supply closet and peered through the crack in the door. His focus fell on the petite figure tucking red strands into a loose wind-blown braid. Every inch of him throbbed, from his heart to his hard-on. He adjusted the inseam of his stiff new pants to suppress his arousal before it raged out of control.

She will not get to me...she will not get to me...she will not get to me...

When the mantra failed to do its job, he counted backwards from a thousand...then stepped out of the closet ready for business with newfound clarity.

Although he kept Lily in his peripheral vision, he paid her no special attention, not even bothering to say hello.

She probably wouldn't recognize me anyway.
Or would she?

A new self-imposed challenge set him off again, but Nick curtailed his runaway thoughts by counting the stack of informational material.

She will not get to me...

He handed a pamphlet to each person with a quick, generic greeting.

By the time he got to Lily, his rebellious libido

was feeling frisky, and the mantra slipped his mind.

She reached for brochure blindly, not bothering to lift her head.

Nick refused to let it go, even when she tugged, forcing her to look up. "Hello again."

She blinked hard before the startled expression faded into a wry smile and a blush bloomed on her fair skin.

Electricity rippled from his eyes to his thighs. It happened so fast no one else could have noticed the invisible energy between them.

What the hell am I doing? She's too young for me.

Instead of feeling like a dirty old man, he felt nothing but hot and bothered.

"Hi." Her powdery voice floated past glossy lips. A wide, million-dollar smile lit up her lovely face, brightening the entire world as far as he was concerned, making it impossible to tear his eyes away.

"What about *me*?" The woman one seat over huffed with impatience that jolted him back to reality.

What about you? Nick glowered at the occupant in the next chair, dressed like she was going to the bar rather than here to learn CPR. "Good afternoon, ma'am," he said with a consolation grin that seemed to satisfy her for the moment.

"I'm Britney. And you're a new face, aren't you?" A knock-off of his bottle-blonde ex-wife wasted no time making casual conversation. "Call me anytime if you wanna go out for a cocktail. I'll show you 'round town."

"Okay everybody," Maresca said, "Settle down. Let's get started so we're outta here on time."

Nick shuffled the certificates on the desk, putting Lily's at the bottom of the pile on the clipboard. And Britney's on top.

"I'm Chief Maresca, as most of you know. This is Captain Nick Knight, our newest member, on loan all the way from upstate New York. He's gonna take you through CPR, which stands for cardiopulmonary resuscitation." He winked at Nick. "They're all yours. I'll be back in a jiff."

Nick turned on the video, giving him ten minutes to regain his composure.

Even if Lily might be into older men...

Well, he didn't wanna think about it. Although he couldn't forget the nineteen-year-old hottie he'd scored with on his thirtieth birthday—not the noblest of choices, but he had been still drinking heavily at the time.

Things were different now. Better. Because he was living sober. And he wasn't looking to mislead any more little girls into thinking he was some kind of Prince Charming for the night. Although being in love with the right woman might be the answer to his prayers and problems.

When the video segment ended, he asked, "Does anyone have any questions?"

Britney raised her hand, wiggling red-tipped fingers in the air. "Where upstate are you from? 'Cause I know people up there."

"He means questions about CPR," a woman cackled, and the class burst into laughter just as Maresca limped back in and mouthed to Nick: *What the hell is going on in here?*

Nick shrugged, grateful for the chaos that turned his rigid flesh into Jell-O.

The chief rolled his eyes, grabbed whatever he was looking for, and stepped out again.

"I'm from Star Harbor. Across the Long Island Sound, by Connecticut," Nick said over the ruckus.

A man's voice interjected, "Come on already. I wanna get outta here on time. You'll probably find him at the pub, Brit. You can pick him up there."

Britney hissed at everyone. "Oh, shut up." Then she flashed her eyes at Nick with a coy smile. "Can't blame a girl for trying."

"Look folks," Nick shouted over the chatter, "this course doesn't make you an automatic doctor or anything. What you learn today will help you in case your family or friends have a heart attack. Situations you might encounter at the dinner table. A wedding. Your kid's soccer game."

After finishing the two hours of stop-and-go videos, he did a quick CPR demonstration with the mannequins.

When it was time to let the class try, he couldn't take his eyes off Lily, down on all fours in front of her victim, with palms in perfect nipple-alignment, arms in good form, ready to push on the chest cavity. A magnificent vibration flowed through him at the sight of her heart-shaped bottom raised high in the air. He wanted nothing more than to get behind her and rock the stiff pillar in his pants into her...*Nine-hundred-ninety-nine...Nine-hundred-ninety-eight...Nine-hundred-ninety-seven...*

"Good job everyone. Let's move onto the

Heimlich maneuver..." He roved the room, eyeing the students, sizing them up, looking for a *victim*.

Squelching any guilt, he hovered over Lily with the zipper-fly of his Dickies in direct alignment to her pouty lips, making him twitch like a compass needle pointing at the North Pole. This might be his only chance to get this close to her, and he couldn't pass up the opportunity. "How tall are you, miss?"

"Um, five-ish."

"Perfect. Could I use you for a minute?"

She hesitated with wide-eyes, like a proverbial deer in headlights.

"You could use me," Britney offered, drawing a dirty look from Lily.

"Oh, fine." With reluctant eye-roll, Lily joined him in front of the class.

"I promise it won't hurt a bit. Okay, folks. I'm six-two. And Lily is only *five-ish*. Imagine she's choking. I would—"

"Let her choke," Britney mumbled under her breath; Nick ignored the crude comment.

"I would bend to her height, and put my arms under hers, and reach around level to her belly button..." As his hands skimmed Lily's waist, he inhaled her fragrant lavender-scented hair. "Don't worry, I'm not being fresh, it's just for the demonstration."

"I'm not worried. I don't go out with firefighters anyway." Her soft words were like a hard kick in the crotch.

"Liar—you *used* to go out with a fireman," Britney whispered, and Lily's body tensed in the circle of his arms. The makings of a catfight stirred the air, but Nick kept moving forward.

"I grab my fist like this...and by pushing in and up I force the air from her lungs and hopefully dislodge whatever's in there." He made the motion a few times.

"Any questions? No? Okay. You can relax." He put his hands on Lily's shoulders and pushed her stiff arms to her sides. "Now, imagine I'm the one choking. Unless she stands on a chair, she's not gonna get her arms around me in the right spot. What would you do?" He looked down into her sparkling eyes, wishing they were alone, a million miles from here. Or at least in the privacy of the storage room where he could taste those luscious lips—he'd change her opinion about dating a fireman for sure.

Lily shrugged and moved behind him. Nick looked over his shoulder at the horrified expression on her face as she calculated her reach-around would align with the waistband of his Dickies.

"As you can see, she'd be doin' the Heimlich on my belt buckle, which won't work."

"I'll do the Heimlich on your belt buckle." Britney laughed, followed by a wave of snickers from the class.

Maresca returned just in time to miss another razz from the audience.

Nick put his back against the wall and pulled Lily to face him. She was shaking under his fingers. "Don't worry. It's part of the demonstration."

Her pretty smile was gone; in its place was a tense line. She wouldn't look at his eyes, which worked fine for him, because he couldn't avoid staring at the hard beads straining inside her tight shirt.

"In this position, she can lean into me, and by pressing the right spot, she could do the same job, using the wall for leverage. Also, I won't crush her if I lose consciousness. So, there are other ways of doin' the same job. Don't think just because there's a size difference it won't work."

"See, ladies, it's true, size doesn't matter." Maresca laughed at his own joke.

Lily made beeline for her seat once the show was over.

They breezed through the AED portion during the last thirty minutes.

"Once I call your name, get your certificate, and you're free to go. Good luck, and I hope you never have to use it."

Nick grabbed the clipboard and started with Britney.

"I have the rest of the day off if you wanna meet me down at the inn for that drink." She snatched the certificate with a suggestive wink.

In the past, Britney's sultry bleached-blonde Barbie doll type might have sparked his interest, but as he matured, his tastes changed.

His sights were set on a ravishing redhead.

If it were true, and Lily didn't date firemen, maybe he'd be the one to change her mind.

However, by the time he got to the certificate he'd saved for last, Lily Lane was nowhere in sight.

Chapter Three

Eight days dragged since Lily stood before Nick with her palms on the hard wall of his abs, while her heart hammered in her chest.

To make an awkward situation a million times more uncomfortable, Britney—that *bitch*—just happened to be there, dropping her snarky two-cents. What nerve—flirting with Nick in front of the whole class, making the rumors of her being a *call girl* even more believable.

Lily wished she could erase that whole day from her mind.

Just when she thought meeting her perfect Prince Charming had been sheer serendipity for a change, she realized it was just another one of life's cruel jokes.

Geez, of all things, why'd he have to be a firefighter? Why couldn't he have had a safe job? Like a librarian. Or a podiatrist. Anything but a firefighter.

The more important question now was how to forget him?

No matter how hard she tried, she couldn't drive that sexy beast from her head. Whoever said *out of sight, out of mind* didn't know what the hell they were talking about.

All the aggravation over one man wreaked havoc on her nervous system. It killed her appetite and triggered a constant dull headache. She'd been functioning on aspirin and coffee for a week, and it finally caught up to her.

Today, in the barbershop bathroom, she puked twice then rinsed her mouth out by eating the peppermint Starlight candies Sophia kept in a crystal dish on the counter beside the cash register.

The only reason she felt a teensy bit better now was because it was almost closing time. She'd be home soon enough where she could jump into bed with her dependable dildo to give her libido a workout.

Last night, when the batteries died during a make-believe play-date with her dream-lover, she wound up polishing off a bottle of champagne to drown the disappointment. She made a mental note to stop at the drugstore and pick up a value pack of D-batteries...

The doorbell jingled, and Lily nearly jumped out of her skin, hoping it might be Nick. But it was just the deliveryman dropping off packages.

"Did it come?" Bob pointed shears at his wife.

Sophia glanced over her reading glasses. "Did what come?"

"The *whatsitcalled*? The heart attack machine."

"AED machine." Lily untied her apron and tossed it into the hamper with a swish.

Bob gave her a curious look. "If you're so smart, where's your certificate?"

Lily clammed up wishing she hadn't said anything at all. She'd fled the classroom to avoid confronting Nick. Consequently, she'd neglected to take her certificate.

"Maybe she didn't pass," Sophia chimed in with a smug smile.

"Of course I passed. Maybe it's lost in the mail. I dunno. If you don't believe me, why don't you call the firehouse?"

The bell jingled once more as the deliveryman stepped out, and in came another burst of cold air along with two last-minute customers.

"Well, well, well, now we can straighten this out," Bob said. "We're wondering where Lily's CPR certificate could be."

"I dunno," Chief Maresca's familiar voice boomed. "But you can ask him."

Lily's eyes nearly popped out of the sockets when she saw the six-foot incubus of her dreams. *Stay cool, just stay cool.*

"This is Nick Knight. He's my new guy." The chief made the round of introductions. "Lily, you remember Nick, dontcha?"

Lily nodded; it was all she could do. Her mouth went dry, and her coolness melted away into a pool of liquid heat between her thighs. Her rapid-fire pulse resonated like a faraway hollow drumbeat in her head. The world rushed at her face in a disorienting red hot and blue time warp. Blinking hard, her vision turned gray before shrinking to the size of a suffocating pinhole.

Then.

Everything.

Went.

Black—

Chapter Four

With the department SUV's siren blaring and lights flashing, Nick and Maresca followed the ambulance with Sophia and Bob in the backseat.

"Stick around, will ya. We're gonna check on Lily."

"You got it, Chief." Nick took a seat in the emergency room lobby that reeked of disinfectant and looked just as sterile and uninteresting as the one in Star Harbor. He grabbed the first magazine from a stack on the end table and flipped mindlessly through the glossy pages.

At first, Lily's fainting spell seemed like a good act. If he was sure of one thing, it was women were mental terrorists capable of anything. They could play the damsel in distress at the drop of dime whenever the mood struck. Sometimes for effect. Sometimes for real. Something about stress levels short-circuiting the nervous system like a defense mechanism—the fight or flight reflex at its primordial best.

He'd been married to the best of the best when it came to drama queens. And he'd responded to enough 911 calls to know when to worry and when to walk away from a false alarm.

Lily looked like a pretty healthy female.

However, when she went down, he sprang to her side. Her usual fair complexion was whiter than the pale moon. Even her pink lips had lost their hue.

Thank God, she didn't need CPR. But being unconscious wasn't a good sign.

A couple of hours and a dozen magazines later, Nick was restless for Maresca to emerge with news regarding Lily's condition. With nothing else to do, he reviewed his list of to-dos.

A few fire alarms to test.

A couple of chimneys to inspect.

Then there was the whole Santa-gig.

Overall, it wasn't a lot to handle, and it certainly wasn't rocket science. The hardest part of the job was keeping up with Maresca's ad-hoc requests—until now. This sitting and waiting for an update on her was torturous.

Nervous energy urged Nick to his feet. Pacing gave him something to do. And when he got tired of pacing, he went back to sitting.

Planted in a plastic chair, he watched the clock on the wall. Stifling a yawn, he fought the need to shut his eyes and ran his hands through his hair, pulling at the root to wake up.

The assortment of wounds parading through the door provided better entertainment than any reality TV program and reminded him of his own myriad of trips to the ER.

Besides the routine check-ups from the neck-up from firefighting injuries, most of his visits had been from drunken bar fighting. A few fractured bones. A couple of concussions. And a broken nose, twice. The garden variety of idiotic injuries that went along with binge drinking.

Thank God he gave up booze and found salvation in sobriety.

He was glad not to be the patient this time.

However, Lily was, and that bothered him. A lot.

He didn't have any good reason to care so much, but he did. That bothered him even more.

For the first time in a while, a little itch inside him begged for scratching, and it had him on his feet ready to find the closest pub for a little comfort in a shot of Southern...

Better make it a double...

A triple if he wanted to get Lily off his mind.

He sat back down. *No thanks. Been there. Done that. Blacked out. Passed out. Rinse, repeat.* Those days were over. He'd thank his conscience in the morning.

If he had such good self-control, then why did his moral compass keep pointing at Lily?

Nick recalled all the things the Star Harbor chief had said about using the transfer to get a fresh start in a new place. Maybe she was the reason destiny brought him to this one traffic-light town. At least that's what he'd thought up until the point when she collapsed.

He got up again to stretch his legs, tempted to march behind the ER doors to find Maresca—and Lily—but went out to find some air instead.

There seemed to be a lot more stars hanging in the inky sky over Scenic View than he ever noticed in Star Harbor. He tried thinking more about the sliver of moonlight peeking between the tall bare trees, and less about the slip of a girl laid up in a hospital bed.

He ought to wait in the SUV—at least he could *meditate* behind the steering wheel parked in the dark. A little hand-solo action would take the edge off, killing the need for a drink and sexual release in one shot.

Knowing Lily wasn't well made him feel guilty for having a rock-hard reaction right now. Ever since the moment he laid eyes on the sweet, young thing, all he wanted to do was bury himself inside her. That smoking-hot body and hair like flames. She came off a little shy. He liked shy. Shy made the most interesting challenge.

"Maybe she just thinks I'm some creepy old dude. I'm not *that* old, am I?" He consulted with the universe as a great gust of wet wind rolled off the Long Island Sound, rattling the branches, churning the leaves on the ground. "I take that as a yes." He sighed in defeat and hunkered down, pulling up the leather collar.

He didn't feel like a creepy old guy for being attracted to her. Didn't feel like a jerk while he was *meditating* about her. He felt pretty good, actually.

The question was—what did she feel?

Maybe he misread her vibes. Who knows? There's a first time for everything.

Unsettled and overtired, he went inside, sat in the same stiff chair to wait some more.

Minutes felt like hours.

Hours felt like eternity.

"Hey, Nick, wake up." He heard the voice in a dream before realizing it was for real. It took him a moment to gather his wits before reflexively socking the guy shaking his shoulder. It was a good thing he opened his eyes to see it was Maresca. "Are ya sleeping?"

"Just resting my eyes." He rubbed them with the heels of his hands.

"You mind sticking around here a little longer while I take the Barbieris home?"

"No problem. How's Lily?" Nick kept the desire out of his voice.

"She says she wants to go home, but they're gonna keep her overnight for observation. Once they have her room ready, they'll let you know. Call me and I'll pick you up."

"Is her next of kin coming down?"

"Her parents are deceased. And I don't think she's seeing anyone."

Bob concurred.

Bingo! Fireworks went off behind Nick's bleary eyes.

"Well…" Sophia chimed in. "If you count my nephew in California—I'm setting her up with him. He'll be coming to town for Christmas. He owns *three* beauty salons. He's perfect for her…"

"Sophia," Maresca said gently, "we're not talking about potential first dates."

"Don't listen to her." Bob grunted, taking Sophia by the elbow. "We'll meet you outside, Chief."

"Why dontcha go sit back there with her?" Maresca jutted his jaw in the direction of the ER doors. "The chairs are more comfortable."

"I'm fine right here." Nick slumped against the hard molded plastic and jammed his fists in his jacket pockets.

"Suit yourself." Maresca disappeared out the automatic doors.

Another eternal hour passed until a nurse emerged to confirm Lily had been assigned a room.

Finally, Nick could leave.

But his boots wouldn't budge over the threshold.

Instead, he headed for the double doors to the ER, using his fire department ID-card to bypass security bells and whistle, and peeked into room 314.

She was awake under an ivory blanket, with wires connecting her to a monitor. At least her pallor looked a little better.

"Nick?" The beeping of her heart rate escalated. He deciphered the terror in her wide eyes, like he was the Devil or the Big Bad Wolf. "What are you doing here?"

"The chief asked me to check on you."

Where were his manners? He could have simply asked how she's feeling. Better yet, he could have started with hello. But her elevated vitals threw off his game, making it impossible to read her vibe with the distraction.

"If you need anything…" His unfinished offer sounded hollow, but he meant it. *Anything.*

"I'll be fine." Her small voice was crystal-clear.

That's it? What did he expect—for her to jump out of bed and throw herself at him?

"Yeah, well…feel better." He waited a long silent moment to see if she had anything to add, and when she rolled toward the window he recognized his cue to leave.

Chapter Five

Lily climbed into the back of the hay wagon against her better judgment. It was the Barbieri's idea she chaperone three little kids belonging to a mother too pregnant to take the ride around Brawny's Farm. Sophia put up a convincing argument, while Bob bribed her with a meal.

"Oh, fine," Lily said. Maybe they were right. She had nothing against fun. Plus, free food sounded pretty good now that her appetite returned to normal since she no longer pined for *Whatshisface*.

No more clammy palms. No more paralyzed chest. No more worrying he might magically appear around every corner.

Big deal, he showed up at the hospital. Out of departmental duty, no doubt. Had she known from the start he was a fireman, she never would fell for him as hard as she did.

Besides, she hadn't run into him since. If he was so interested in her, he had plenty of time to say something. He knew where to find her. All that hocus-pocus CPR-vibration must have been nothing but a fluke.

No. Nick Knight wasn't interested in her any more than she was interested in this wagon ride with these unruly mini-monsters.

The jumping, climbing, screaming, fighting was more than she could handle. When they finished wrestling each other, they tossed tiny fistfuls of hay at Lily. It stuck to her lip-gloss, and she spat it out of her mouth.

"Come on, fellas. You better quit it or else I'll tell your mother," she threatened, but none of them listened. "Boys, someone'll get hurt!" Still, no one obeyed. It was a mystery why their parents wanted more of them. "That's enough!" She grabbed them by their hoods and parked them on the seat until the party lights in the distance signaled the end was near.

"Aww," the boys sang in unison.

"Thank God. I'm ready to go home." Lily jumped to the ground, brushing debris from her bottom.

Rubbing her big belly, the mother asked in earnest, "Would you like to babysit sometime? Ten dollars an hour."

Shell-shocked, Lily shrugged a potential maybe despite the urge to refuse with a flat-out no. Sure, the money was tempting, but not at the risk of losing her sanity. Without making any promises, she slipped away to find the Barbieris.

They weren't on the dance floor. Or by the snack shed. Or anywhere else.

The crowd was thinning now that night was coming on, but the lack of light made it harder to tell the shadowy figures apart. She planted herself in a dim corner, watching for Bob's little lumpy body and Sophia's big-bottomed pear-shape.

Stuffing cold hands into the pockets of her puffy-coat, she pulled out remnants of hay. Pointy bits and pieces made its way inside her clothes, too. It was everywhere.

"Hello, Lily." The familiar voice came from behind. Footsteps shuffled closer until his silhouette stood between her and the rest of the world.

She wanted to run, but the blood drained from her limbs, making them feel like cold sand.

Be cool. Just be cool.

She willed the lava leaking in her panties to be arctic glacier-cold. Just when she'd finished agonizing over this person, her treacherous body reacted in the most wicked way all over again.

"Oh. Hi, *Nick*. I didn't see you standing there. In the dark." The last time she saw him he was lurking outside her hospital room.

"How've you been?" He sat beside her at the picnic table.

A small snort escaped, as if she'd actually fall for another heartfelt conversation with the devil in her dreams. Lifting her chin, she steeled herself against his heat. "I'm fine," she lied.

"It's a chilly night. I'd hate to see you get sick. *Again.*"

She wasn't sure if he was concerned or condescending by his teasing tone.

"I said I was fine. Totally fine," she added with a little singsong to her voice to disguise the nervous quiver.

"I know you're *totally* fine." His deep voice dropped a sultry octave the way he had whispered during the CPR lesson. Right in her ear. Right through her soul. "You don't have to tell me twice. One look at you and anyone can see how totally fine you are."

She ignored his loaded compliment, afraid to fall prey to his roguish charm after she worked so hard to get him off her mind.

Caution—he's a fireman.

"So…" Hesitating, she segued onto a less controversial subject. "How's your bungalow coming along?"

"It's coming. I'm still debating if I oughta pull up my roots in Star Harbor and plant them here permanently." He leaned back against the table and propped his elbows like he was getting comfortable. "How's your place? Any biters yet?"

"Nope." Lily sighed in lieu of venting. Talking about would probably jinx any luck she had left. Since posting the For Sale sign in the ground, there hadn't been a single phone call.

"Well, I'm sure it'll sell. You need a little patience. The right person has to come along."

The right person…ha! He was supposed to be her Mr. Right, but she couldn't have been more wrong. Lily snuffed the small talk, allowing the awkward silence to fill the space between them, as she concentrated on the folks on the dance floor.

After a minute, Nick seemed to be the one most affected by it. He leaned his head so close she could smell the cinnamon on his breath. "Lily, did I do something to upset you?"

The party lights softened his features, making him look glorious like the Adonis she recalled from their first encounter. She shook her head, fighting the urge to succumb to the power of his plea. She couldn't allow the frigid veneer she designed to thaw so easy. "It's not you…it's me. I'm just…a bitch."

"No. You definitely are not."

"Yes. I am." She narrowed her eyes and shot him with a laser-look, but he only chuckled.

"No. You really aren't."

Damn this man! She gnashed her teeth before snapping back. "How can you say that? You don't even know me."

"Trust me." He cocked a brow. "I know one when I meet one. And you're not one."

Lily folded her arms over her chest. "Is that so?"

"Yep. I was married to one once, so I know about these things."

Absorbing his words, curious about the details he dropped, she took the bait. "So, what, that makes you an expert or something?"

Nick twisted his torso in such away she caught a whiff of the most intoxicating phenomenal-aroma of leather and musk. She needed to fortify her weakening willpower against this firefighter's potency before her hormones raged out of control.

"As a matter-of-fact, yeah," his voice floated against her ear, "I am an expert. Or something." His arm slipped behind her until his hand appeared on her other side, resting on the tabletop.

Huh? Lily jolted at his overt pass—unless, maybe, she read him wrong yet again, and just he enjoyed playing head games.

"If they were giving out bitch-awards, I hate to tell you this, but you wouldn't even be nominated," he said in a mellifluous tone that made the back of her neck sweat despite the autumn chill. "I'm actually surprised a nice girl like you isn't taken."

Despite her better judgment, Lily prodded the conversation with a husky bedroom-voice she barely recognized. "How would you know if I'm taken or not?"

"Well, when we first met I got the feeling you kinda liked me. I figured if you had a man, you wouldn't be looking at me the way you did...the way you're looking at me right now."

Heat flashed in her cheeks. Grateful for the cover of darkness, knowing how candy-apple red they get when all fired up, she challenged his words despite knowing they were true. "I-I'm not looking at you in any way," she whispered weakly.

"Yes, you are." He surprised her by moving his hand onto her shoulder. She surprised herself even more by letting him. "You can't deny there's a spark between us."

She rolled her eyes, but she didn't shake him off. "You're delusional."

"And you're adorable. Why dontcha let me take you out sometime?"

Lily sucked in a breath, stupefied, her heart wavering. She couldn't say yes—although, Lord knows she wanted to more than anything! She struggled to say no, but the tightness in her throat sealed off her words. After a painstaking hesitation, with a halfhearted headshake, she said, "I, uhh...I don't think so."

To combat the sting behind her eyes, she rubbed them hard, suppressing any impending tears of disappointment. She had a rule. She couldn't—wouldn't—break it. She couldn't risk a broken heart.

"You okay?"

"Twinkle lights make me woozy," she lied.

"You're not gonna pass out on me again, are you?" he asked with concern.

"*That* had nothing to do with you."

"Good. I hate thinking it did. You gave me such a dirty look before you keeled over."

"The truth is I wasn't feeling well that whole day. The doctor said it was from fatigue."

"Yeah, yeah. I know, I know. I just hope you're taking care of yourself. Eating right, getting enough rest. I thought, maybe we can go out to dinner."

"And then what—you'll tuck me in bed?" Tuck rhymes with…God—she nearly made the terrible Freudian slip.

"Tuck you in bed? Hmm." A mischievous smile curled his lips. "I wasn't planning on going there, but if that's what you want."

She cut her eyes at him, and he shut up quick.

"Lily, I'm just kidding. Really. Taking you to bed is the furthest thing from my mind."

"Humph." She shrugged off his arm just as Chief Maresca interrupted.

"Oh, good, you found her." The man was double-fisted with roasted corn and a steaming Styrofoam cup.

"Sure did." Nick nodded.

"The Barbieris had to leave. Sophia didn't feel well. I told them I'd take you home."

Lily didn't have a chance to protest before the chief shuffled away.

"Come on." Nick stood. "Let's get some corn. I'm starving. How about you?"

"No, thanks." She fought the urge to befriend

him after visions of being in bed together bounced in her head. "You go. I'll stay right here."

"Stop fighting it. I'm attracted to you. You're attracted to me. Let's agree on that much."

She refused to budge.

"I'm done joking, I promise. I'll be nothing but serious from this point forward. Now, come on, let's get some food."

Lily still wasn't sold.

"Look, I'm not leaving you here for some other guy to swoop in and snatch you up."

"No one's snatching me up."

"I am. But you're not making it easy, which I completely respect." He smiled and put out his hand.

She felt guilty for putting up such a cold front when he didn't deserve it. "Corn gets stuck in my teeth."

"They make dental floss for that. Now come on, before they shut down the snack bar." He took her hand despite her best attempt to keep her body parts to herself.

"You know what? I think I'm gonna ask the chief to take me home now."

"Yeah, here's the thing…" He tugged her along gently. "I'm the chief's new driver until further notice. So, when he said *he'd* get you home, what he really meant was *I'd* be getting you home tonight. Are you okay with that?"

Dumbstruck, she rambled, "Um, I only live a mile away. I could actually walk—"

He stopped and spun her, putting his face in hers. "I know. I've seen you all over town. But it's dark and cold. I really don't want you walking." He squeezed her biceps, demonstrating his disapproval.

She read the lines of concern around his frown and solemn eyes. Felt it in his voice and under his fingers. Of all the things he'd said and done in the little time she'd known him, this, by far, was the icebreaker to shatter the igloo she'd built around her fragile heart. No man has ever given her an ultimatum before, and as much as she should despise it, it secretly thrilled her.

He thrilled her.

And as much as she wanted to deny it, she couldn't. Consumed by the moment, she forgot about the firefighter, and only saw the virile, attentive man.

"I-I didn't say I would. I-I said I could."

"Well, don't even think about it." He pulled her securely under his arm as they sauntered toward the snack shack.

Eyeing the selection, he asked, "See anything you like?"

Besides you?—she smiled in private.

Hot apple cider fragranced the air, making Lily's mouth water, along with an array of seasonal treats. Jelly and caramel apples. Apple cobblers. Apple pie. Kettle corn. Roasted corn. Corn bread. Pumpkin pie. Pumpkin bread. Pumpkin muffins. Chili. Clam chowder. And more.

Although the aromas were tempting, her hunger pangs vanished. She shook her head. "Nothing for me."

"Not even a hot cider? It's medicinal on a cold night."

"Oh, fine."

"Spiked or straight?" asked the fellow behind

the counter.

Nick glared questionably at Lily. "Better make 'em straight. Alcohol won't help you recuperate from *fatigue*." He gave a perceptive smile, and his inflection made her feel stupid for the diagnosis, but they probably didn't have a medical code for lovesick. "Candy apple?" he said.

She'd kill for one but wasn't about to gnaw on something so sticky in his presence. Plus, without dental insurance, she couldn't afford more than an annual checkup. "No, thanks. I've gone this far with zero cavities and plan on keeping it that way."

"Don't mind if I have one. And a bag of sugar nuts. A couple of caramel lollipops. And candy corn. It isn't Halloween without candy corn." He handed her the nuts and filled his jacket pockets with the loot like a kid robbing a candy store.

"You've got a little sweet-tooth, huh?"

"You're right about that." He cocked his head and winked, grinning like the Big Bad Wolf at a scrumptious Red Riding Hood.

His sexy smile made her twitch, sending a wave of scalding cider over the side of the cup.

Nick must have shared her little earthquake, because he fumbled with his apple and it landed on the ground before he took a single bite. "Oh, well." He sighed in disappointment.

Lily sighed too—only hers was more of the swooning kind, studying his movements as he bent down in fitted jeans to pick up his dirty apple, then strutted to the trash barrel with it.

They strolled along, sharing the nuts, sipping hot cider under the strings of lights.

"You have straw in your hair, you know." He plucked it out and showed her.

"Hay."

"Hey, what? I'm not making fun of you. I'm just letting you know."

"I know. But that's hay, not straw."

"I'm no farmer, but I think it's the same thing."

"Well, it happened on the hayride, not the straw ride." She shut up fast, feeling silly for arguing over something so trivial and for lacking anything clever to say.

"Must have been one helluva hayride."

"I was babysitting. Doing a favor for a pregnant mom with three boys who needed a chaperone."

"Sounds like fun."

Lily grimaced. "It was awful."

"So, I guess offspring are outta the question then, huh?"

"What's that supposed to mean?"

"Nothing. Just making conversation." He shrugged in a haphazard way it was almost believable.

"Oh, *really*?"

"Sure. I'm just asking where you stand on the subject, that's all. No biggie. I could have asked about the weather. Or politics. Or religion. But *you* brought up the subject of children."

"Uh…I dunno. What do you think about 'em?"

"I think they're great."

"Well, these kids were a handful."

"Then start with one. See how it goes. And move on from there."

"Who—me?"

"You? Me? We?" He released a sneaky smile she couldn't decipher.

No doubt, he was messing with her head, but she went along with it anyway, reacting with a playful backhanded slap to his gut. "I don't think I'm cut out to be a mother."

"I think you're wrong," he added before quickening his pace.

Lily stopped dead in her tracks. Staring at his back, caught between confused and captivated, the thought of making a baby with this beguiling man was tempting. But it wasn't an offer—just conversation, like he said.

"Hey," he called back, waiting for her to catch up. "Wanna check out the corn maze?"

"No. Not really."

"Why not? You scared or something?"

Lily shrugged. "Maybe."

"Of me? Or being in the *spooky* maze at night?"

"Both."

"There's no reason to be afraid of me, Lily."

"I'm kidding. I just don't like corn mazes. I'm not afraid of anything." She raised her head and thrust her chin forward, neglecting to mention her fear of debt collectors, being broke, and potentially homeless at the velocity of her financial plight.

"Then why won't you let me take you out?" He unleashed a killer smile that left her weak and tingly all over. "I'm not asking to set a wedding date. Just one date. As friends."

The idea of going out with him was so enticing she almost agreed without considering the consequences. She didn't want to say no, but she was afraid to say yes. So, she bit her tongue and said nothing at all.

"Never mind." He waved the words away.

Her heart shriveled. "Nick…"

"Pretend I never asked. Let's just enjoy the moment. I don't like corn mazes either. I was just hoping for a chance to use my manliness to protect you. Change your opinion about going out with a firefighter."

"I have nothing against firemen." Spilling her soul crossed her mind, but beyond rejecting his invitation after the loss of his candy apple, she didn't want to ruin the night any further.

"But you just won't date one." He smiled with his lips, but it didn't reach his sad eyes. "Or you just won't date me. It's all right. I'll get over it. Eventually."

She didn't have the heart to admit he was right. This conversation was the hard and fast reminder she needed to instill the golden rule she almost broke. Firemen were off limits. They can only break your heart one way or another.

If she couldn't date a firefighter, maybe she could be friends with one.

They wandered along the perimeter of the party, where the crickets were louder than the music, chitchatting about everything and nothing at all.

The chief reappeared, startling her. "They're closing up shop soon. I'm ready to go whenever you are."

Now that she was getting to know Nick better, she didn't want this night to end, yet it wasn't fair to lead him on. "Me too," Lily lied.

"Let's hit the road." Nick whipped out a big key ring and twirled it on his finger.

The ride in the backseat was uneventful, with the static of the sports-talk radio station and the chief's directions on how to get to her house on Sunflower Summit.

"Did Nick tell ya? He's our new Santa Claus this year," Chief Maresca said.

Her heart fluttered at the idea of him sticking around for the next two months. "Good luck."

"What's that supposed to mean?" Nick glanced in the rearview mirror.

"Oh, nothing. Everyone loves Santa. I'm sure you won't have *any* trouble." Lily grinned at the mental picture of him dressed as the man in red.

"What do you mean—*trouble*?"

"You know, some kids carry grudges for not getting what they wanted last year."

"Don't listen to her. She's messing with you. We have nothing but respectful kids around here. They'll love you. Just don't make any promises Santa can't keep."

When they pulled into the driveway, Nick got out and opened her door. He hung his hand on the roof and lingered like he was waiting for something more than just her to slide out of the backseat. Her phone number, perhaps?

Under the bright streetlight, his dark eyes were a friendly-ferocious combination, which gave his features an edgy air of danger. *This is what he must look like at the end of a date. Smoldering. Kissable. Irresistible.* She wasn't accustomed to this breed of masculinity.

"I'll see you around," he whispered in the wind, and she wanted to say she hoped so, but not in front of the chief.

She ran to the door with headlights shining behind her until she was safe inside.

Peeking between the drapes, she watched the red taillights until they were out of sight. Maybe out of sight, but never far from her mind, not since the day they met.

Was she completely out of her mind for considering, even for a single second, getting involved with this man?

With her fingertip, Lily wrote the answer on the foggy glass. "Yes."

Then, recalling her mother's advice, she swiped the word away with a swift fist and an excruciating, "No!"

Chapter Six

Lily's unrelenting refusal to go out with Nick gave a *mile-wide stubborn streak* new meaning—wider than the Long Island Sound. She played hard-to-get with a competitive edge. He was tempted to toss her over his shoulder caveman-style. But waiting her out was the better plan, so he dug down deep for the patience to endure the ride.

To take his mind off the rejection, he'd immerse himself in work. A few chimney inspections and fire alarms remained on the list. And a first aid class was coming up. There was plenty of time to get his mind around the Santa role.

Once he did what he had to do, he could do what he wanted to do, which was thumb through the brochure for his custom camper. He hadn't been this excited since getting the new plow for his truck last year.

And he hadn't been this excited for a woman in…forever.

The bunkroom was empty most nights, so it was almost like having his own place. But it was *nothing* like his own place since he couldn't invite a lady over. Not that he had anyone in mind other than Lily, and she wasn't budging.

A few more weeks and it'll be here—the

ultimate Christmas present he dreamed of since he was a kid. Even more so during the past few years as his mid-life crisis started creeping up early.

But that's what happens when you're married at twenty-two and divorced by twenty-four.

What's worse is stuck in a relationship with your ex-wife because she's your best buddy's sister.

Tristan swore he never reported Nick's business to Claudine, but he *must*. How else did she keep getting his cell phone number every time he changed it? The psycho-bitch popped up on his caller ID but never left a message.

Thank God he didn't have kids with her.

But they did share a godchild. And for that reason alone, he felt obligated to be civil to her on the few annual occasions they saw each other.

Thinking of bitches…it was laughable that Lily considered herself one. If she only knew Claudine, he bet she'd laugh. too.

Sweet little Lily—she was probably a tiger in bed—Tiger Lily.

He'd felt larger than life, wandering around Brawny's with her petite frame tucked under his arm. It was hard to control his fantasy of bending that curvaceous *bod* every which way.

Maybe he was the crazy one thinking a nice girl like her would want to date this lonesome loser.

Wait a minute—this lonesome loser's worth some buku bucks!

Maybe if she knew about his money she'd change her mind. Then again, he didn't want the bankbook to be the deciding factor in his love life.

She didn't seem to mind the age-gap, which he

anticipated would be the bigger issue.

The only problem appeared to be his job.

But she was just getting to know him. There was still time to tally up his flaws. A recovering alcoholic with an unpredictable ex-wife may be pushing the limits.

Quitting the fire department might make her happy. But what about him? His job made him feel better about himself. He liked helping people. Nothing felt as good as saving a life.

Well, next to making a life.

Making love.

Imagining a tribe of little redheads running around had his wheels turning.

Crossing her path was a wake-up call. Maybe thirty-six wasn't too late to start a family. Sure, he was older, but he wasn't *that* old. There were probably a few good swimmers left in his sperm count. If Charlie Chaplin was having kids until he was eighty, then Nick could probably pull one off by forty.

Before he could sway her into making babies, he needed to convince her to go on a date…

It was a shock to be thinking such things after being a devout divorcee for so long.

But it felt good, like he found a new hope for his life. And the funny thing was it had nothing to do with the money.

He didn't want to mess things up with Lily. A girl like her needed some time. Some wooing. Some coaxing. Some special persuasion. Now that he'd decided he wasn't going anywhere anytime soon he could do things right.

But then he remembered she was.

The conversation about selling her house replayed in his mind.

It was on the market. It was a burden. She wanted to relocate to Manhattan.

Once she sold it, she'd be gone...

An incredible idea curled his toes: *Buy the house and give it to her for Christmas.*

It was a perfect plan.

But if it didn't work and she didn't fall for it, he could always blame it on Santa Claus.

Chapter Seven

Lily was hungrier than a pilgrim on Thanksgiving. She hadn't been to the grocery store lately for anything more than bread, milk and eggs, so when she tore through the kitchen it was no surprise to find the cupboards and refrigerator bare.

She could have celebrated with the Barbieris, who put out a feast for every holiday, but she hated feeling like a charity case around their perfectly happy extended family. She skirted the whole scene, blaming it on an imaginary stomach bug, topping off the lie with a fictional fever.

The truth was she felt too crummy to be socially polite, in no mood to put on the happy face and make annoying chitchat.

Thinking of annoying chitchat, luckily, she hadn't run into Nick in weeks since the night at the farm.

Saying yes to his plentitude of offers had been tempting, and saying no was getting harder. She could have agreed to go out as friends, but with the way her heart rate soared in his presence, being buddies would be tougher than simply going off his radar.

"It's for the best, right, Ma?" She rolled her eyes to heaven, ignoring the brown water-stained blotches on the ceiling, then glanced at her sickly expression in the bathroom mirror.

Even if Nick's hazardous occupation weren't an issue, no doubt, once he got past the basic getting-to-know-you boloney, he'd grow bored. A mature man like that wouldn't stay interested for long with her quicksand of debt and lifetime of emotional baggage.

What good could come from a single date? Except for wanting another one. And another...

Like he said, he wasn't setting a wedding date.

Lily snorted at her reflection. "As if." *No way, no how,* she refused to fall for a firefighter, no matter how much she wanted this one.

The empty pit of her lovesick stomach groaned, encouraging her to throw on some clothes before foraging for food in town. No velour ensembles today as all her good tracksuits were in the dirty laundry pile. Instead, she pulled on some mismatched oversized sweats that doubled as winter pajamas.

Being home alone on the holidays sucked. They were always the hardest days without her folks, and she wondered how many more she'd have to endure. Maybe it was time to revisit the therapist she'd seen after her mother's accident. Instead of getting better each year, she felt worse.

To counter the grief, she walked. Long walks. Power walks. Meandering strolls. Whatever it takes to clear her mind. If she focused on other things, neutral things like the weather or nature, sometimes she could forget about being so lonely.

All bundled up, Lily headed outside.

It was like stepping into a time machine.

One whiff of pungent chimney smoke reeled her back to her early childhood before life took a nosedive. The familiar fragrance didn't affect her any other day. Only certain holidays got her so choked up she couldn't see straight. A fresh fire on Thanksgiving was more memorable than the smell of roasting turkey.

It was probably a good thing the memories with her dad were short and sweet, otherwise she'd have more to miss.

Next to the crooked For Sale sign at the end of the driveway, screaming squirrels scurried around the old maple tree where crows cawed from the canopy of branches. Withered leaves fell like rain, twirling in the breeze, swirling around her decrepit little house. Once a snappy shade of colonial blue with a sharp looking red door, it was now just a faded eyesore.

Her life started falling apart the day her father died. But when did the house start falling apart? Shingles fell off in different places during Hurricane Floyd in 1999. The broken windows were the originals since the 1960s. The irreparable crack in the foundation had been there since God knows when. There wasn't any way to fix the shack up without tearing it all down first.

Maybe if her father were alive he would've taken care of it before it got so bad.

Maybe if her mother hadn't opened up and over-extended the credit cards using Lily's name they could've afforded the basic repairs.

None of that mattered now as she was too far behind on the mortgage to ever catch up. A buyer better show up soon before the bank foreclosed.

Even more reason to find a new job.

Although the Barbieris depended upon her, they couldn't pay her any more than what they already were, and tips were slim when business was slow.

She swiped a tear and sucked back the sadness, shaking off the pains of her past.

Walking ought to release enough endorphins to improve her dreary disposition, as ominous as the opaque sky.

Almost everything was closed on Thanksgiving, so her choices were limited to grabbing a bag of beef jerky at the gas station's mini-mart or daring to go into the dreaded diner. She didn't like eating alone in public, which worked perfectly because she didn't have enough cash for the bill, plus a tip.

Studying the Specials posted on the glass door, she debated on ordering something to go. She could eat it at a picnic table in the park.

A man's thick voice behind her shook her deep contemplation. "Going in or coming out?"

"Sorry." As Lily jumped aside to free up the doorway, she recognized Nick's superlative smile beaming like the sun, warming every cell in her body. His nose was rosy, and his quizzical eyes shimmered with moisture as if he'd been in the frigid wind for too long. She bit her tongue to prevent any wild thoughts from rushing past her shivering lips.

"Hey, are you following me?" He winked.

"I, um…" His distinctive musk and cinnamon scent derailed her train of thought. She hid her smile while brushing away an escaped curl tickling her chin. Did her best to contain the butterflies fluttering in her belly.

"*Well*?" Nick cocked his head. "I'm cold and hungry. How about you?" He grimaced, underdressed for the blustery weather in a black leather jacket with a red scarf tucked into the collar. "Care to join me?"

Of course, she wanted to join him but the rapid fire of her treacherous heart made it difficult to breathe, let alone talk, and her feet were too stunned to move.

"You don't have to if you don't wanna. But why eat alone when we could eat together? Unless, of course, you're not here alone."

"I...I'm not here with anyone."

"So, how 'bout it?"

Giving her conscience a swift kick into the corner of her crowded mind, Lily hoped her mother wouldn't be too disappointed. It's only one meal. Surely Mom wouldn't want her to eat alone on Thanksgiving.

She fought the urge squeal in delight and released a half-hearted sigh instead. "Yeah. Sure. Why not?"

"Really? I don't wanna twist your arm or anything."

Guilt tweaked her heart as his wounded eyes touched her soul. "You're not. It's just..." She shook her head, debating if this was a bad idea or not. She hated how easily he ruined her confidence with his heartbreaking smile. "Nothing. Never mind."

"It's not like a date or anything, if that's what you're worried about." He sounded cautious. Oddly, the more insecure he seemed, the less self-conscious she felt. "You can write it off as two friends bumping into each other at the diner, okay?"

Although she should be glad he was still working the friends-angle, Lily's heart plummeted.

"Yes, of course…friends. I'm just surprised to see you, that's all."

"Well, I hope it's a good surprise."

Every fiber of her being screamed, *Great surprise!* But she refrained from admitting it. Instead, she continued to stumble over her mixed emotions, hoping nothing idiotic poured from her mouth.

He held the door wide for her. "After you."

Sorry, Mom. Lily prayed to the darkening sky before stepping over the threshold.

Once inside, her stomach clenched from hunger as an aromatic wave of everything delicious hit her; she could almost taste the fragrant feast in the air.

Overheating under the bulky clothes, she pulled off her gloves and shoved them in her pockets. She kept her hat on and head down, hoping to go unnoticed, especially when Britney beelined in their direction.

"Well, well, well. Looky here. If it isn't Captain Knight. Remember me, from CPR class. I haven't seen you in here once, the whole time you've been in town."

Nick shrugged. "I usually call for delivery."

"Would you like to see the Thanksgiving Specials?" Britney cocked her hip. "I can have 'em wrap it to go."

"We'll just take a booth in the back."

"*We?*" Britney's eyes bounced from Nick, down

to Lily hiding in his shadow. "Oh. My. *Gawd*. Don't tell me you two are together? Follow me." She sauntered in tight orange pants that made her big ass look like a pumpkin. "Your waitress will be right over." She handed Nick a menu with a whisper, "Let me know when you're tired of playing with children, I have a fire you can put out." Then she tossed a paper menu wrapped around a pack of crayons and sneered at Lily. "What's the matter—can't find any brats your own age to play with?"

Lily refused to respond. It wasn't worth losing her cool over Britney. At least not in front of Nick. She held her breath, waiting for her rival's heels to fade away.

"Didja steal her boyfriend or something?"

"Seriously—you think I could steal a guy away from her?" Lily hitched a thumb over her shoulder.

"Sure, why not? She's hot, but...I like my girls sweet. What's her problem with you anyway?"

"I don't want to talk about it."

"Come on...You can tell me."

"No. I can't. Just forget it. Okay?"

"Oo-kay. But if you change your mind, just let me know. I'm all ears." He flipped open the menu. "So, what'll it be?"

"You know what? I'm not so hungry." Confronting Britney was an instant appetite suppressant.

"Seriously?" He blinked and closed the book. "What's wrong? Maybe I can help."

"Nothing's wrong. It's ancient history and doesn't stop repeating itself. I'll tell you some other time—like in a hundred years."

"Do you wanna get outta here?" Nick poised to slide out of the booth.

It would be worse to leave and let Britney think she won, than to stay and just suck it up. Lily didn't want anyone accusing her of being a spoiled high-maintenance baby. "Do you mean outta town? Or the diner?" She joked with a small smile, but they both fell flat.

"I meant the diner—but I can see why you might wanna skip town."

"Forget it. I'm fine. I'm used to her. She's no big deal. I'll just have, um…a hot chocolate."

"Really?" Nick gave her slanted look. "That's *it*? Hot chocolate."

"Yeah." She waved it off and finally shrugged out of her coat after a bead of sweat trickled between her shoulder blades.

"Fine." He nodded, peeling off his jacket and scarf.

Lily winced at her reflection in the polished silver accent décor. Lost inside the oversized marble-gray sweatshirt, her figure looked similar to *Jabba the Hutt*, while his fitted charcoal-colored sweater accentuated the biceps budging beneath. What a mismatched combination they were.

"Hot in here, huh?" Nick dug his fingertips into his collar, stretching the neck hole.

Not as hot as you.

"So, is this how you usually spend Thanksgiving—in the diner?"

Escaping for a long walk sounded too weird and would probably generate more questions she wasn't in the mood to answer. "Not really. This is a first. I usually spend it at home. Alone."

"Yeah. Me, too. I can live without the family drama."

When the waitress appeared with two glasses of water, Nick ordered for them both.

"Two hot chocolates, please..." Heat flared in his eyes as he asked Lily, "You sure that's *all* you want?"

She thought of a dozen things she wanted—all of them required scrubbing her brain with soap. "I'm sure."

"That's all." He dismissed the waitress, and at the same time his cell phone rang a sick song from inside his pocket, but he didn't answer it.

"You just said you were hungry." Lily halted the server. "Wait a minute please."

"I can't eat in front of you while you just sit there watching."

"Give me a break. You can eat whatever you want."

"*Whatever* I want?" His devilish smile spread slowly, making Lily's skin tingle. "Well, then, can we add a few big cookies?"

"Cookies and cocoa," the waitress confirmed before walking away.

"Sounds like the Santa Claus diet."

"We're grownups. Whose gonna stop us from eating cookies for dinner? I'm sure we can find a bite to eat later. Maybe hit the mall, too."

"You gotta be kidding." Lily giggled. "It's Thanksgiving. The stores are closed."

"The radio said they're opening at midnight for early *Black Friday* shopping."

"I don't go near there on a regular day, never mind Black Friday. Shopping's not my thing."

"I thought it was programmed into the female-chromosomes—the shopping gene."

"Nope. Not this female." It was much better excuse than venting about being broke.

"Do you wanna come with me?" His voice dropped an octave, making a trip to the mall sound so seductive she couldn't say no. Made her wish he'd ask the same question in her bed.

"We'll see."

"Aww, come on. I'd like to get Chief Maresca something more than a bottle of scotch for giving me the job."

She sighed, tapping her nervous fingers on the tabletop, getting the feeling he didn't take no's very easily. "Okay, fine. But don't say I didn't warn you. I guarantee the mall will be a zoo, and you'll wish you listened to me."

"Probably."

The waitress delivered steaming mugs of cocoa overflowing with whipped cream and marshmallows alongside a mountain of cookies—a bunch of rainbow squares, an oversized black-and-white, and a few linzer tarts. She left the check, which Nick paid in cash on the spot.

"Hey." She reached into her bag and took out some crumpled singles. "I owe half."

"Put your money away." He gave her the same look as he did when he told her not to walk home from Brawny's farm, so she put the money back.

After they gobbled the cookies, he pointed to her cheek. "You have some crumbs...right...there."

She swiped her chin with the back of her hand.

"Almost...over more. It's still there. Here, let me help you." He reached across the table and wiped them away with his thumb, leaving a sizzling trail where skin touched skin.

It wasn't the first time he put his hands on her, but it was the first time she saw stars in his eyes, staring musingly at her lips, making her lick them on impulse.

"Um, thanks." She dropped her chin to hide the secret crush blooming in her soul. Could he sense the puppy love? Could he see it in her eyes? She needed to change the subject before she said something outrageous regarding her unraveling emotions. "So, tell me...how'd you get stuck playing Santa Claus this year?"

Nick chuckled. "Well, let's just say the chief's a pretty persuasive man."

The chief's not the only one.

Chapter Eight

"A little early for a snowplow, isn't it?" Lily asked, as Nick directed her toward his silver pickup truck, parallel parked across the street.

He skipped the details regarding his compulsion to mount it right before Thanksgiving, in time for the first snowfall, and simply said, "What can I say? I like being prepared."

"Just like a boy scout." She smirked, climbing inside.

"Kinda." He chuckled, slamming the passenger door.

They meandered around Scenic View on a guided tour through Lily's sentimental eyes. Her topographical knowledge of dirt roads, backwoods, and dead ends beat his GPS system's incorrect interpretation every time.

He shared his pack of cinnamon gum while she shared her opinion of the local territory. From Alphabet Town Preschool where she spent her formative years, to Zhang's Chinese takeout where they made her favorite spring rolls.

"See that building on the right?" Lily pointed to the abandoned-looking warehouse, next to a gentleman's club called the *Devil's Oasis*, as they passed the marina, heading uptown toward the railroad station. "Doesn't look like much, but that's the *Sound System* recording studio. *Broken Zipper* made their first album there. Just a little Scenic View claim-to-fame," she said with a haughty twang.

Embarrassed to admit he never heard of the band, he nodded and smiled anyway for effect. "Oh, wow, that's cool."

The more he learned, the more he liked—about her, and this place.

"What's with all the junk?" She referred to the stockpile clanking around in the backseat anytime he turned a tight corner or made a hard stop.

"Just stuff. Spare clothes. Work gear. You know, the usual."

"The usual?" She poked her nose over the seat. "I don't usually keep an *axe* in my car."

"You mean the *Halligan bar*? It's a forcible entry tool. Never know when it'll come in handy."

She shot him a dirty look, then turned her head and crossed her arms.

"My job really bothers you that much, huh?" He made a mental note to clean out the backseat *Asap*. If, by chance, she went out with him again, he didn't want to spoil it with reminders of why she refused to date him in the first place. "Please don't let it ruin the night, okay?"

"*I'm* not letting anything ruin the night," she hissed, as pissed as a rattlesnake.

"Then smile, will ya?"

"There. How's that?" She flashed a fake smile before pouting again. "Happy?"

"Come on, Lily. I thought we were past all that."

"Me too. Guess I'm not. Seeing all your gear... I

don't want to think about it…it's so…dangerous." She glared at the windshield, not giving him the consideration of looking him in the eye.

"So, what—you want me to take you home now?"

"Why? You *wanna* take me home?" She unsnapped her seat belt. "You know what—I can walk from here."

"What the hell are you doin'?" He yanked her elbow and swerved off the road onto a patch of dead grass. "Are you nuts?"

"You're breaking my arm."

"Better than letting you break your neck."

"I'm not jumping out. I meant drop me at the corner. You can let go of me now."

He released her with a deflated sigh. "What are we fighting for?"

"I dunno. Let's just forget it."

He put the truck in Park. "No. Let's finish it, now. You hate my job, and you won't date firemen—I get it. That's why I haven't made the effort to see you." He hesitated, gathering his thoughts, not mentioning how he staked out her place and followed her downtown today. He was tired of wasting precious time with childish games. "Whenever I see you, it makes me wanna see you more."

"Well…if we're spilling our guts, the truth is I've tried hard to forget you. I thought time and space would get you off my mind, but it didn't work. Every time I see you, we connect…or maybe it's just in my head. All this talk about life, and us, and everything…I don't want to get so far ahead of myself thinking this could go somewhere. Who knows when we'll run into each other again after today?" She calmed down and put on the seatbelt.

All he got out of her rambling, he summarized in a whisper, "You tried to *forget* me?"

"Sorry...but, yeah, I did. Let me tell you, it's not easy." She bowed her head, shielding her face with the collar of her coat.

"Is it just because I'm a firefighter? Or does it have anything to do with me being so much older?"

"Nick." She shook her head. "Age is a number."

"Lily, I'm thirty-six. And you're—God...you're not even close." He shook his head, disgusted by his lustful intentions.

"That doesn't bother me. I lived through more than most people my age. Twenty-four's not as young as you think."

"So, it's just my job you have a problem with?"

She shrugged. "It's not that I have...*a problem*. It's...it's hard not to imagine something bad happening in your line of work."

"I'm sorry you feel that way."

"You don't have to apologize. That's not what I'm looking for."

"Then, what are you looking for?"

"I-I don't even know any more." She sighed like there was something else to say.

"You still wanna go home?"

"No."

That was all he needed to hear as he put the truck in Drive and tore down the road before she changed her mind. He circled around town, killing time, taking the long way up steep hills and down winding roads.

They cruised past the Scenic View Inn, decked out with the most holiday flair, covered with icicle lights, miles of garland, and giant bows.

Coasting past Town Hall and the Center Square, he whispered, "Whoa," at the sight of the huge Christmas-Star-of-David menorah-tree.

"Pretty, right?" Lily exhaled dreamily.

"Pretty impressive."

"Turn here." She pointed to a side street—a private road that didn't register on his GPS.

Behind wrought iron gates and manicured landscapes, McMansions on the bluff overlooked Scenic View Harbor. Each miniature castle was dressed in full holiday grandeur, more remarkable than the next. Nothing gaudy or over-the-top here. No plastic Santas. No reindeers on rooftops. No inflatable snowmen. Just classy crystal lights like tiny stars outlining the fine architecture.

"Whaddaya think? Nice, right?" She stared out the windshield, while Nick studied her profile in the ambient light.

"*Stunning*," he breathed.

Lily must have caught him staring from the corner of her eye, because she gave a shy smile with fluttering eyelashes. "Um, if you follow the bend we'll wind up on Main Street."

They rode a few miles on North Shore Road until the shopping center was in sight.

The empty parking lot meant one thing—she was right—*The. Place. Was. Closed.* A few people were setting up chairs in a line at the front door of Child World. Other than them, no one was here.

Lily's wide eyes spoke volumes: *I told you so.*
She popped a Starlight in her mouth. "Want one?"

Nick shook his head, grinding his teeth on a
piece of flavorless gum. He pulled up against the
curb to ask the organized mob what time the mall
would open.

"Five," said a random voice.

"Minutes? Or hours?"

"Five in the morning," another voice chimed in.
Meanwhile, his cell phone moaned again, and he
dumped the call.

"Why don't you just answer it already?" she
asked sweetly, her curiosity laced with a tone of
genuine concern.

"'Cause I don't wanna!"

"Oo-kay." Lily shifted closer to her side of the
bench seat.

"Sorry. I didn't mean to snap at you. I know who
it is—my ex-wife."

"Maybe she has something important to say."

"Then she can leave a message. I don't wanna
talk about her," he grumbled, driving toward the exit.

"We can wait in line if you really want to do
this."

"Ah, *fuggetaboutit*. There's plenty of time 'til
Christmas. I just thought, you know, we could spend
some time together. When I was a kid, that's what we
did on a date—go to the mall."

"I thought you said this *isn't* a date." Her
seriousness made him wish he chose a different
word. Then she smirked like she was just messing
with him. "We're not kids, Nick. We can go
anywhere we want." The husk in her voice vibrated

all the way to his core, and he swallowed hard, not sure what she was thinking behind those motel eyes.

His itchy fingers twisted the radio dial, searching for something Christmassy and corny enough to restrain his fantasy from running wild.

"Wait!" She grabbed his hand, sending another shock through his system. "Go back—I love that song!"

"Dontcha wanna hear holiday music?"

"No, thanks. '*Hell-ooo. I've waited here for you. Everlong…*'"

The green light turned yellow, then red. Nick tapped the brake. When he came to a full stop, he took his attention off the road for the moment to gaze at her as she bopped to the beat, feeling the passion of the song as she sang along with the Foo Fighters.

"'*And I wonder…*'" The song continued, but Lily stopped and stared like she was reading his thoughts.

"What?" The sensitive serpent trapped in Nick's jeans twitched as if she was some kind of snake charmer.

"Nothing. Just thinking," she uttered at the guitar bridge.

"About?" *And I wonder…*

"About this song. This day. You. Life. Everything." She released tangible energy, making Nick want to pull over and grab her on the spot.

The light turned green, and he pressed the gas.

"*And I won-der…*" David Grohl sang.

Thank God for red lights and redheads.

At the next intersection, he timed his arrival with the stoplight so he could lock eyes with her for another *ever-long* moment, then he manipulated the rest of the ride home to last as *ever-long* as possible.

"I didn't mean to waste your time going to the mall. That was a stupid idea."

"You're not wasting my time, Nick." She reached over and put a reassuring hand on his sleeve. "Don't even think it for a minute. I'm sorry about before. I really would like to get to know you better. You seem like a *really* nice guy. Any girl would be lucky…" She bit her bottom lip.

"I don't want *any* girl, Lily." He made a sharp one-handed turn toward Main Street that sent everything in his backseat sliding to one side. "And I really don't wanna take you home yet."

"We can park somewhere if you want."

He sucked in a hopeful breath. "You sure?"

"Yeah."

"How about the marina?"

She nodded with a delicious grin. "Sure."

"Okay then…"

He drove until he found his usual out-of-the way spot where he liked to *meditate* about her.

Being here with her now seemed strange. Just the sound of their mingled breath and the hum of the engine. They stared out the windshield at the moon brightening the sky, reflecting off the water like a sea of twinkling diamonds. Hypnotic waves lapped against the dock, making everything seem to sway.

He'd done this sort of thing plenty of times, on plenty of *first-and-only* dates in Star Harbor, but it never felt like *this*.

"Are you warm enough?"

"Too warm." She slipped off her coat and shoved up her sleeves. She wore no rings. No bracelets. No chains around her neck. Not even earrings. Most girls wore some piece of jewelry, but Lily wore none, and it thrilled him, creating the illusion that she never belonged to anyone else.

"Lily…" His attempt to break the awkward silence didn't get very far, not with her glittery eyes staring at him. "I haven't done anything like this in *so* long. I forgot what it's supposed to be like."

"Me, too."

"Let me ask you something. What exactly are you looking for?"

She broke her gaze with a few rapid blinks. "What do you mean?"

"I'm wondering…about what you said before." He shrugged, not even sure what he meant. "Outta life? In a relationship? From *me*? In one breath, you let me know I'm un-dateable. And in the next, you tell me any girl would be lucky…I dunno what to think. I just wanna know what you really want."

"Hmm...I guess what any girl wants—I just…I want it *all*."

"Good to know." Satisfied with her blanket-response, he stole a first kiss. Harder and deeper than he intended because he was working on limited self-control.

Lily purred, bowing her pliant body against him.

His arms wrapped around her, grabbing the hair at the nape of her neck to pull her against his mouth. Like yin and yang—a perfect fit, a perfect kiss. She tasted every bit as sweet as he imagined. Like a candy cane, only better. He slid the bench seat back and pulled her across his lap, cradling her head in the crook of his arm, to kiss her deeper, harder, longer.

Ever-long.

She squealed.

He pulled away to survey her face for any hints of uncertainty, relieved he saw nothing but a molten stare that matched his own raging temperature. "Did I hurt you?"

"No. Not at all." Her face was red and raw from his five o'clock shadow working overtime.

He stroked her hot cheeks with the side of his finger, holding her face like some fragile treasure. The moonbeam illuminated her profile, setting her delicate features aglow.

"You're okay with this?"

"It's fine. I'm fine. Really. Everything's *fine*." She nodded with eager eyes.

"Then I'm gonna kiss you again, okay?"

"I hope so." She wet her lips, but he moved around them to nibble her neck, her jawline, her ear lobe, making the glorious moment last.

"You are so delicious." He murmured between kisses. "I can't get enough of you." The words slipped out as easy as the oversized sweatshirt slipped off her shoulder.

He could have undressed her without even trying, but his plan wasn't to seduce her in the truck, even if she wanted it. She deserved their first time to be somewhere better than his front seat. Besides, the glove compartment was empty; he'd tossed away the remaining condoms figuring they'd expired after being in there for so long.

"I-I…" Lily gasped. "Nick, I can't have sex with you. Not here…now. I'm not—it's just—I can't. I'm not ready to go that far."

"Shh…it's okay. I wasn't even thinking it."

She pulled back with skeptical lust-drunken eyes. "Yeah, right."

He brushed the hair off her feverish forehead, tempted to kiss those luscious lips again but needed to adjust his jeans before they cut off circulation to his crotch. "I can use some air. How about you?"

"Sure, why not."

He opened the door and got a cold, damp blast in the face, then went around to help her out of the passenger's side.

"Better put your hat on." He tugged it over her hair. She zipped her coat halfway, but he dragged the metal tab up to her chin. "Didn't you have gloves?"

"I don't need them." She jumped out and put her warm hand in his. "It's f-f-freezing. Are you s-s-sure you wanna d-d-do this?"

"It won't be so bad once we're moving." He pulled her closer to benefit from the protection of his body against the whipping wind. "Which way should we go?"

She tugged him in the opposite direction of the Scenic View Inn and any chance of renting a room there for the night.

The stores were all closed along Main Street, but their holiday lights sparkled in full festiveness, making it feel more like Christmas than Thanksgiving. No traffic tonight. Just a few pedestrians. Other than that, it was like having the whole town to themselves.

They strolled by Violet's Valise, a lingerie shop in a purple Victorian-style building. Nick slowed the pace to browse the window dressing.

"Those mannequins are a helluva lot better looking than ones we use for CPR training, dontcha think?" Two wore sheer red and white nighties with feathery trim. The third had painted-on silver pants and a shimmery camisole.

She grabbed his elbow. "Let's keep going."

"No. Let's wait for them to open in ten hours." He wrapped her in his arms. "We'll start a line."

Suddenly playing coy, she shooed his hands away. "Quit it."

He didn't let her get away so easy. "Why ya being so shy? I'm only teasing. I don't like this stuff anyway."

She rolled her eyes. "Yeah, right."

"No, really. I prefer cotton and fleece over satin and—what is that?" He pressed his face to the glass. "Silk or something? Who likes that stuff? Give me some sturdy rayon or a polyester-blend—now *that's* a fabric I can get into."

"You're crazy." She laughed.

"Crazy about you." He kissed her forehead. "But I'm serious. I especially like my underwear fireproof."

"Well, then, there's nothing in Violet's for you."

"What about you?" There was plenty that would look good on her. Better yet, scattered on the floor.

"There's nothing for me either."

"That's not true." He rocked her in a slow dance on the sidewalk. "I wanna take you shopping there sometime. You don't have to get anything too—"

"*Slutty?*"

"I was gonna say revealing."

"But you mean slutty."

"There's nothing wrong with slutty."

"Oh, really? If you like it so much, then maybe you should go after a girl like Britney. She seems interested in you, in case you didn't notice."

"Yeah, I have noticed. But she's a little too *aggressive* for my taste. There's nothing wrong with wearing something a little slutty, as long as you're wearing it for me and no one else."

"I don't think so." She pulled him away from the window.

Nick's stomach growled as they approached the aromatic air emanating from diner. "Hungry yet?"

Lily flashed incredulous eyes, then glared through the glass where Britney stood behind the register. "Uh, no, thanks. I'd rather starve." She quickened the pace.

"Are you sure you don't wanna talk about it?"

"Talk about what?" She snatched her hand away.

"Aww, come on, Lily." He stopped in the crosswalk, caught her shoulders, and spun her to face him. "You can tell me what's up with you two—why she has it in for you."

"She doesn't like me 'cause I dated her brother. Years ago. In high school. I don't like talking about it—same as you don't like talking about your *ex-wife*." She grinned smartly, zapping him where it hurt, and he took the bullet, not wanting to upset her by pushing the issue beyond the comfort zone.

At the sight of oncoming headlights, Nick nudged her across the street.

She stopped in front of Mr. Lucky's door as some patrons stumbled out, bringing the warmth with them. "Want to go in?"

"Wouldn't you rather keep walking?"

"Just one drink."

With a low, reluctant groan, he pulled the door handle for her. "Sure. Just one."

It was dark and jam-packed with post-Thanksgiving partiers. The hot, rancid air was a repulsive alternative to being wind blasted, but she wanted to come here. He couldn't refuse.

She seemed to know where she was going, quickly cutting between cliques, maneuvering through the throng. He kept their fingers laced, not letting her slip away.

He hadn't been inside a tavern in years, but the layered odors were the same. Stagnant cigarettes and stale beer mingled with the garden variety of heavy perfume and potent cologne. However, this place had the hint of something more pleasant, like burning trees.

Claiming a vacant table for two next to a wood burning stove built into a brick wall, she let him pick sides. He slid into the booth with his back to the wall facing the mob. She sat across the lacquered tabletop, staring at him, making him self-conscious.

"Well?" Her green eyes glowed.

"You come here often?" It wasn't supposed to sound like a line, but it did.

She shook her head. "I haven't been here in a while. But this is still the best seat in the house."

"What'll ya have?" he asked before the waitress appeared.

"Hmm?" She sighed thoughtfully and sat back, stripping off her hat and coat, adjusting her baggie sweatshirt. "A scotch." She wrinkled her button nose.

"And a cherry soda on the side."

"Scotch, huh? Wow." He expected her to order champagne since she bought it by the caseload. "I'll have a seltzer."

"That's it—really? If I knew you weren't drinking I woulda just ordered the soda."

"It's okay. You can order whatever you like."

The waitress returned in a jiffy, and Nick paid on the spot, not bothering to open a tab.

"I don't like it." Lily took a taste of the amber liquid in the short glass and winced. "I'm only drinking it to get warm."

"That'll do the trick."

"Want a sip?" She pushed it toward him.

"No, thanks."

"You'll put your tongue in my mouth, but you won't drink from my glass. Go on, take a sip."

He slid it back. "No. It's not that at all. I'm...cutting back," he said, treading carefully into the dark depths of his unflattering past.

Cutting him a suspicious look, she sipped her scotch in small medicinal increments, scrunching her face with every taste. "God, this stuff is gross. I dunno how people drink it for fun."

"I know. I used to be a *big* drinker." He cringed as he let the bones of one of his ugly skeletons out of the closet, waiting for her to bolt straight for the front door.

But, surprisingly, she stayed.

"So, you don't drink any more—at all?" She sounded concerned.

Nick shook his head. "It was getting too hard to handle. I knew if I didn't get hold of it, I'd be dead or a lifetime lush." He sighed, liberated now that he released the big guilt-laden secret.

"Sorry, we can leave…"

"Don't worry about me. I'm okay. Trust me. I'm over it. I know my limitations. I can be around drinkers and not wanna drink." He exaggerated his willpower.

"You sure?"

"I wouldn't have come in otherwise."

She slammed what was left in the glass and said, "Well. I'm finished, so we can go."

"Warm yet?"

"Yes. Hot, actually."

"Takes the edge off, doesn't it?"

"Sure does." The sharpness in her glassy eyes seemed to melt away, her invisible protective armor fading fast.

"Enough to wanna talk?"

"If you don't mind me having one more, I just might tell you anything you want to hear."

Nick flagged the waitress. "Make it a double."

"So, how do you want it?" She looked at him lopsided. "Quick and dirty? Or slow and painful?"

"Huh?" His head nearly exploded. "You changed gears without me—are you talking about?"

"Sex?" She giggled. "Nooo. I mean my story."

He checked his wristwatch in jest. "Hmm, I have plenty of time. The only place I need to be is in line at Violet's in nine hours."

"You're sure you really want to hear it?" Her softening gaze washed over him.

Nick felt the warmth in her eyes, but longed to know the heated history inside her head. Playing it cool, he swirled the straw in his tall glass while his knee riveted a mile a minute under the table.

"Yes. Of course." He couldn't avoid sounding eager.

"I don't even know where to begin." She blew out cheeks full of air, then chased a nip from the scotch with a sip from the straw floating in the soda.

"My mother, she was, um…an alcoholic." Lily stumbled over the words as if speaking an alien language. Her eyes fell from his to her fingers laced around the scotch.

"She was sorta the infamous town drunk—well, not sorta. She *was* the town drunk. But she wasn't always like that. She only started drinking outta control after my dad died in a fire, saving someone's life. I was only four, so I don't remember much, except…it changed everything."

"I'm so sorry." It didn't begin to cover it, but it was the best he could do after being sideswiped by her words. Now he understood why she didn't date firefighters. Why she refused to date him.

She gave a small, gracious nod. "Yeah, well, my mom—she never got over it. So, as you might imagine, my home life was pretty…erratic. And then there was Mark, Britney's brother. We'd known each other since elementary school."

Her voice grew small and her eyelashes moistened with hard memories.

"We dated on and off throughout high school, but…his family never approved of their only son dating the local drunk's daughter. That didn't stop him from seeing me. He never told his family about us. But my mom had known all about him. The two of them got along great, actually. She didn't mind him staying over all the time. She joked about how nice it was to have a man around the house again. He mowed the lawn, took out the trash and stuff, and she bought him beer. Things seemed good for a while. Then, one night she was walking home from the bar. A car hit her." Lily shrugged with a downhearted sigh.

"*Tsk*." At the sight of her wounded eyes, Nick's insides flinched although he kept his body stoic. Shaking his head in disbelief, he had no idea the girl lived through such tragedy. The night in the ER, when he asked about her next of kin, Maresca didn't mention any of these painful details.

She drew a shaky breath before continuing. "She was crushed between the bumper and a tree. Mark's family was pissed because he came with me to her funeral rather than go to our graduation ceremony. I inherited the house. And the bills. Mark sorta just moved all his stuff in little by little. I wasn't in the frame of mind for a serious commitment, but I didn't want to live alone. Just because we were sleeping together, it didn't mean I wanted to marry him. We'd known each other for so long, it seemed like my only option. I dreaded the idea of meeting anyone new. Unloading all this information on someone else— like I'm doing right now. I figured it would drive any decent guy away. Mark already knew everything about me...about my life. We never talked about being in-love. It wasn't romantic, just convenient. I said yes because I didn't know how to tell him no after sticking by me all that time." She stopped to breathe then swiped her nose with the heel of her hand.

Nick wished he never made her recap this horror story. At least she trusted him enough to talk about it. If she gave him the chance, he'd fix things for her—or he'd die trying.

"Aww, Lil…" He took her hand. "I don't even know what to say."

"I know." She studied his palm, tracing the lines. "There is nothing to say. That's why I'm not a big drinker. I know how bad this stuff is for you. I'm only drinking now because…well, you have me so nervous."

"I don't want you to be nervous around me."

"That came out wrong. I feel comfortable…I'm just nervous that someone will…" She dropped off with a sigh and flashed damp eyes to the ceiling like she was saying a silent prayer.

"See us together?"

"I don't care what people think. I just worry about Bob and Sophia finding out I played sick to get outta their Thanksgiving invitation. I hate hurting their feelings. They're like family. But…it's not the same as *real* family."

"You've known them a long time, huh?" He sounded like a therapist, and felt like one, too. But he didn't mind. As long as it was helping her, he'd be whatever she needed.

She nodded. "My mom worked at the barbershop for years before I was born, before she even met my dad. Then I started when I was old enough to push a broom. I was already on a career path, so I never planned on college. I worked toward my beauty license, taking occupational classes in high school.

Mark didn't do much, but drink beer, play video games, and take up time and space. He didn't want any part of his family's diner because his sisters gave him grief about being with me. Eventually, I gave him an ultimatum—get a job or get out. He wound up working at the pizzeria and volunteering in the fire department. He planned on taking the New York City Firefighter's exam despite my feelings..."

"At least he made an effort."

"I know. That was why I couldn't kick him out. I was hoping he'd go quietly, you know?" She strained to hold back the tears. "So, I accepted his engagement ring, even though I knew I shouldn't. And things were okay for a few weeks after that. Then, one day, as he picked me up from work, he got called to a fire on the other side of town. I offered to walk home. But it was the middle of winter. He wanted to take me to the firehouse so I could drive his car. He was going too fast and swerved to avoid hitting a kid running across the road. We slipped on a patch of ice and hit a pole. The next thing I know, I'm in the hospital with a broken arm, cracked ribs, and a concussion. Mark was DOA. Brain hemorrhage. I was a mess after that. Felt guilty as hell for everything. Britney said her brother would be alive if he weren't with me. I guess I sound like a real jinx, huh?"

Nick sat there stunned, thinking he could use a drink himself. He took the almost-empty scotch from her fingers. One more sip and she might start blubbering, as she rightly should, but not here, not now. Not in front of Britney who just sauntered in as the bartender announced, "Last call."

"Hey, come on. I'm ready to get outta here." He stood, helped put on her coat, and led her through the crowd.

Before they could make it out the door, Britney stepped in Nick's path. "Hey, Captain Knight in shining armor. How about a drink?" she slurred with her breath reeking of wine. "Oh. My. Gawd. Who let *you* in here?" She sneered at Lily. "Isn't it past your bedtime?"

Lily dodged Britney to reach the door.

"You better watch out." Britney caught Nick by the elbow. "That girl's an accident waiting to happen."

Lily held the door open, letting in the chill. "Come on, Nick, please."

The patrons complained in unison, "Shut the goddamn door."

Every second Lily was alone outside, the further she could go, the harder she'd be to find.

Nick tugged free from Britney's tight fingers, pushed through the door, and caught up with Lily across the street in front of the post office.

"I wish…" she panted, pacing, "I wish I could just get far from this place. Far from her!"

"Relax, will ya. Who cares what she says?"

"I can't relax." She tripped in the wrong direction.

"We're parked this way." Nick grabbed Lily's hand, guiding her to the truck, then opened the passenger side and helped her climb in. But before he could shut the door, she started weeping into her hands. "Easy. Take it easy. It's okay."

He offered his hand to squeeze, but she swiveled

in the seat, grabbed his neck and wrapped her legs around him while she cried against his leather collar.

The wind beating on his back did nothing to cool the hot blood surging to his groin. He hoped she couldn't feel his swelling arousal.

"Shh...everything's okay." It damn well wasn't okay. But he'd fix this. He just needed to know what was going on.

The sobbing soon tapered off to sniffling. "I'm okay."

No doubt, the alcohol had something to do with her breakdown. It probably played a part in her suckling his neck. Her hot breath moistened his skin as her lips moved across his ear, nibbling the lobe before rubbing her tear-soaked cheek to his. "I'm okay. But I know how you can make me feel better."

As guilty as he felt about enjoying her booze-induced affection, he didn't stop her. He felt like Superman with her in his arms, as if he could save her from anything.

"Kiss me, Nick. Kiss me *hard*."

He should have pried her off, but her words were a command he couldn't refuse.

Enveloped by her limbs, he grabbed her bottom; she was light enough to carry. He pulled the tailgate down one-handed and set her on the edge. Then darted back inside to dig through the gear for the fire blanket, itchy but good enough for a makeshift cocoon.

He unzipped his jacket so she could nuzzle against his sweater rather than the stiff, cold leather. Her palm skimmed over his nipples, down his abs, until she cupped his groin with feather-light fingers.

Yes. His eyes rolled back, and he stifled a moan. But her earlier words echoed in his mind. *Not ready. Not here. Not now.* She deserved better. He didn't want her regretting anything, ever, so he grabbed her hand, brought it to his lips, and kissed her knuckles.

"Dontcha wanna finish your story? Maybe if you talk about what happened, you can put it behind you, and it won't hurt so much. Maybe I can help you."

"No! I can't. I know if I do, you'll hate me."

"Trust me, I could never hate you." He wanted to tell her he loved her but it was too early to use such definitive terms. "Whatever happened can't be that bad."

"I can't. I just can't." Glossy eyes screamed her desire for him to know everything, but her lips refused to budge.

He figured she just needed a little push in the right direction.

"Lily, whatever it is, I think you'll feel better once you put it out in the open. Otherwise, it'll never stop hurting. I can't help you if you don't tell me. Look how easily Britney pushed you over the edge. Why give her the power to hurt you? I'm giving you the power to let it go. I'm not gonna judge you if that's what you're worried about."

"No!" She shrank against the wall of the truck bed.

"Listen, you need to tell me, otherwise..." He sighed heavyhearted. "Otherwise, I don't think this will work out between us. Whatever it is that bothers you so much, it won't go away, and it'll always be a big question mark in my mind. I'm not gonna be able to stop thinking about it until I know what hurts you so much."

"It's time for me to go home." She shoved him away and leapt over the tailgate like an escaping animal. "I'll walk if you don't want to drive me."

"Lily! Lily, wait. Of course I'll drive you home." He shouldn't have pressed so hard, but how could he fix the situation without knowing the whole story?

He parked in the driveway, and before he could come around to open the passenger door, Lily jumped out and ran into the house without even saying goodbye.

Chapter Nine

It was a quiet day at the barbershop. Lily spent most it leaning her forehead on the cold glass door, hoping to spot Nick cruising by in his silver pickup or tooling around in the red SUV. Propped in this position for nearly two weeks now, she needed to get out of the pathetic funk before Sophia dragged her to the doctor.

She hadn't heard from him since the Thanksgiving debacle and doubted she ever would again. Not unless she sucked it up and apologized.

Apologize for what?

Remembering how he pushed her to the point of tears with his need-to-know nonsense started a new wave of disgust. She didn't want a therapist, although she could use one.

She wasn't even sure she wanted to sell her house any more. Especially since Sophia kept giving her a dirty look, trying to convince her it was a bad idea.

Lily wasn't sure what she wanted any more, and she was tired of waiting for the pieces of her life to fall into place, rather than fall apart as they usually do.

When she wasn't pining for a glimpse of Nick, she was holding her breath for the realtor to call with some good news. With her fingertip on the foggy glass, she calculated the dollar amount she might walk away with if the best offer came through, but she couldn't figure it out. As long as there was enough money to clean the slate, she'd be satisfied.

"Lily?" Bob put down his newspaper. "You okay?"

"I'm fine."

Sophia came over and put the back of her hand to Lily's forehead. "Maybe you should go see Dr. Kramer just to be sure you don't have mono or the flu."

"I just have a lot on my mind."

Sophia snorted. "Maybe it's just guilt for putting your house on the market. Your parents would be so disappointed—"

"Mind your business," Bob grumbled on his way to the bathroom.

Sophia went back to filing her nails behind the cash register. "Your parents' memories are tied to that house. Why don't you let us help you with the bills if you're having money problems?"

"I don't feel like talking about it right now." Lily slumped in the chair wishing she were anywhere but here.

"Do you want to talk about what happened on Thanksgiving?" Sophia tapped the file against the desk expectantly. "You said you were too sick to come over, yet I heard you were at the bar with some *man*."

It was only a matter of time before the news filtered to Sophia's ears. "His name is Nick."

"Not that *fireman*."

Lily nodded.

Sophia threw her palms in the air. "What about Bruno? He's coming in a few weeks. I told him you wanted to meet him."

"No—y*ou* want me to meet him."

"Is something going on with the two of you?"

"No!"

"How old is he anyway?"

"What does it matter? He's a good person. And…and I like him. A lot."

Sophia's eyes widened. "*And?*"

"And *nothing*. That's it." Lily bit her tongue to keep her emotions from escaping into runaway words. "There's nothing more to tell. We're just friends."

"Well, I hope you're not making *friends* with the wrong kind of man. I don't want to see you get hurt…like your mother." Glancing toward the ceiling, Sophia recited a quick prayer under her breath and made the sign of the cross.

"Would you please just stay out my business?"

"I'm only thinking what's best for you."

"I know—and I appreciate it. I really do. I'm sure Bruno is great and all…"

"Sophia!" Bob returned to his chair. "Leave the girl alone. If she likes Nick, she likes Nick. This isn't your decision. The heart knows what it wants. Stop trying so hard to play matchmaker. We are *not* her parents. Only she knows what is right for her. She didn't ask for our advice. So, let's keep our opinions to ourselves."

"*Roberto Alfonso Barbieri*, I cannot stand by and let someone I love set themselves up for failure."

"I'm sure Lily can handle this without our help."

"Sophia…" Lily broke in, hating to be the cause of such animosity. "I *do* want your help. I love your help. But not with this. I want to do this on my own."

"Kill me for caring too much." Sophia snatched her coat from the closet sending the hanger flying off the bar. "I'm going to get coffee. Want anything?" She stomped out before Bob or Lily could answer.

Bob grabbed Lily's elbow before she dashed after Sophia.

"Let her go. She's upset over something else, not just you. You're just getting the tail-end of it."

Seeing the weary lines on Bob's plump face, Lily realized she wasn't the only one with issues. "Is everything okay?"

"I dunno—I hope so. Our daughter came for Thanksgiving *without* her husband. She says they're getting divorced. She wants to move back to New York with the kids and stay with us, but our condo is too small. She'll have to find an apartment. A job. The boys'll have to change schools. Sophia has a lot on her mind. And she needs to learn to keep her nose out of everyone's business, even if she means well."

"Sorry, I didn't know."

"So, you like this man—Nick? You think he could be *the one*?"

Lily half-shrugged and nodded, barely able to look Bob in the face as they discussed her romantic life. "I dunno," she lied.

"I know Chief Maresca likes him, so he must be a decent fella."

"He is."

"So what's the problem?"

"Besides his job." It was easier to blame it all on Nick's career than on herself for being too embarrassed to talk about her history.

Bob shook his head. "What happened to your father was a terrible thing. It doesn't mean it's going to happen to Nick. Sure, his job's risky. So's crossing the street. You can't stop lovin'—just like you can't stop livin'."

"I know. You're right. But it's not just the job." She released a pent-up sigh. "We seemed to get along so great—I was ready to forget everything my mother said about never dating a fireman. Then he wanted to talk about stuff from my past. And I-I didn't. I wasn't ready. Not that night. It was too soon—for me anyway. You know what I mean?"

Bob's nodding head indicated he knew well enough.

"But he kept pushing and pushing. I was afraid I'd say something to drive him away. So I freaked out instead. I haven't seen him since Thanksgiving."

"Lily, everyone makes mistakes."

"I know, I know. It's probably for the best. I should never have gotten involved. I'm not ready for a real relationship anyway."

"It's okay to need time. Things that are worth having don't happen overnight."

"Well, he didn't seem to need much time. He spilled his guts about everything. I tried, but couldn't. He thinks I don't trust him. I'm just not ready to give all my secrets away yet."

"If he's a real man, he knows trust and love take time. We call 'secrets' for a reason, otherwise, we'd be bragging about them. Everyone has them. We don't become old and wise without being young and foolish first. You're a good girl, with a good heart. If he's not crazy about you by now, then there's something wrong with him."

"Thanks Bob." She reached around his thick midsection with her head against his chest, breathing in his Old Spice, recalling what it was like to hug her dad, which made the tears already flowing come twice as easy.

Bob pried her off after a moment. "No more crying, okay?"

She nodded.

"You know what?—I'm still waiting for that heart attack machine to come. It's December already. Why's it taking so long? Would you mind stopping by the firehouse to find out when it'll be here? Someone could have a heart attack and drop dead on my floor. That someone could be me with all the drama around here these days. Go on and take your time."

****

Nick sat behind Maresca's desk fielding phone calls while the chief spilled scotch into two empty coffee mugs.

"How about getting into the Christmas spirit with me?"

Lord knows a drink was just what Nick wanted and the last thing he needed. He hadn't told Maresca that he was *livin' la vida sobria*, because, well, he didn't think it was worth mentioning. "No thanks, Chief. I'm good."

"Come on, will ya? 'Tis the season. You better get your jolly on. Smile a little. Start getting your mind around the role."

"Don't worry. I'm just tired. And my back is killing me, that's all."

"Well, I keep telling you to get a little apartment or something. A fella can only spend so many nights in the bunkroom."

"You ain't kiddin'." Nick did a few neck rolls and shoulder shrugs to work out the kinks.

"By the way, I ordered lunch."

"Great. I'm starving. Whatja get—pizza? Chinese?" Nick's mouth watered, his empty stomach growling for something more satisfying than this morning's cup of coffee and buttered bagel.

"Nah. I went with good old burgers and fries. Bad for the heart, good for the soul. I got you the Super Deluxe with extra bacon and cheese, no onions. I'm picking up the tab—you can pay the tip. Now, if I can just find *The Suit…* It's gotta be around here somewhere," Maresca said before continuing his mission.

The man was right about sleeping on the cot. Nick's back was out of whack from the lack of lumbar support. He was getting too old for this. The slip of paper with the phone number got washed with the jeans, so he never called about that room-for-rent.

He swallowed some aspirins stashed the chief's desk drawer and chased it with the last swig of coffee in the Styrofoam cup.

Reviewing his to-do list, aside from playing Santa Claus, there was only one item left, one name not in compliance with the fire code—*Lily Lane.*

Damn, he missed that girl. He had the

everlasting ache in his groin to prove it.

He ought to be professional and complete this one last chimney inspection, but he felt stupid approaching her, considering how he ended things Thanksgiving night. A disgusted grunt escaped at the memory of telling her to talk or walk. He didn't blame her for running away full speed.

Maybe he'd do a drive-by one of these days to apologize for being a bastard. He regretted dropping the ultimatum like he really meant it, playing the tough-love psychoanalytical Mr. Fix-It.

But he didn't regret the kiss, though. It was too good to regret. Too good to forget.

Was it too late to ask for forgiveness?

Probably.

He called the real estate attorney again and left a message with the secretary. "Double her asking price. I don't want anyone else to get it. And push to close in time for Christmas. Leave an open-ended move-out date with an option to rent…"

It was a slick plan.

Either she'd hate him more for being so sly.

Or she'd love him twice as much.

He hung up with newfound glory gushing through his veins just as a feminine voice jolted him to awareness.

"Got a special delivery for ya." Britney's slinky body hugged the doorjamb, dressed in a silver fur jacket, giving him a faux salute with red manicured nails that matched her lips.

Nick glanced at her, trying to read her vibe considering the last time he ran into her, with Lily, was the root of all his recent troubles.

"Hungry?" She jutted her hip and flipped a cloud of white-blonde hair over her shoulder.

Was she referring to herself? Or the brown paper sack in her hand reeking of the chief's extra crispy onion rings? Nick kept his mouth shut.

"I haven't seen ya 'round town." She came in and closed the door with her hip. Dropped the bag on the chair, and parked her rear on the edge of the desk with her short skirt hiked up like an open invitation.

Between Britney and her noxious perfume mixing with the greasy, oniony odor, Nick suddenly lost his appetite.

"I've been busy."

"I hope Chief Maresca isn't working ya too hard. Where is that man anyway?"

"Around somewhere." He kept his eyes glued to the clipboard.

"Mind if I wait here? I'll just have myself a little bit of this and keep you company until he's back." She flicked her gum into the trashcan, picked a mug off the shelf, and poured some scotch.

"Maybe you could take your drink and wait somewhere else."

"Geez. You don't have to be so rude."

"I'm not being rude." Nick turned his attention to shuffling random papers he pulled from the bottom drawer, attempting to appear swamped. "I've got a ton of work to do."

"You go right ahead. I won't stop ya. I just wanna say goodbye to the chief."

His curiosity piqued, Nick took the bait. "Going somewhere?"

"Key West, actually. I'm leaving tonight. My

cousin has a steak house and needs some experienced help. What've I got to lose?—nothing. Might as well give it a shot. If I don't like it I can always come back to Scenic View."

"I *really* hope it works out for you."

Britney drained the cup and poured some more. "I want you to know I have nothing against Lily. We were almost sister-in-laws you know."

Well, it took long enough to mention her name. A sharp pang in his stomach had nothing to do with hunger. Interested in what she had to say, he felt guilty for listening. Thoughts of Lily and Mark together pinched a nerve behind his eye.

"I lost my baby brother because of her." She sighed between sips with eyes welled up with tears. "She even stole my mother's engagement ring."

It took every bit of self-control not to throw her out the door for accusing Lily of such *crap*. He refused to believe she would steal a penny, never mind valuable jewelry.

Whatever the story, he needed to hear it from the source—if she ever spoke to him again. He fantasized about an apology, with some sweet make-up sex if he got lucky.

Nick got tired of hearing Britney's slanderous complaints and decided it was time for this unwanted visitor to leave. She could come back later to say farewell to the chief.

The problem was, she didn't seem to take the hint.

So, he tried the tactic that worked with his ex-wife whenever he wanted to get rid of her—just pull out some cash and poof, she disappeared, like magic,

"Here."

"The chief has a tab at the diner."

"Consider it a tip."

She unfolded the hundred-dollar bill, then smiled. Her cell phone chirped, and she checked the message on the screen. "Oops. Gotta run."

Nick followed her out only to lock the office door behind her in case she returned.

"You sure about this? It's a lot of money."

"Keep it."

She shoved it in her pocket. "Oh, in case I don't make it back to say goodbye, would you give this to the chief for me?" Britney stretched her neck and planted a kiss on Nick's cheek before sauntering away.

****

Lily froze in the hallway at the recognizable voices emerging from Chief Maresca's office. The nasally Long Island accent belonged to Britney. And the owner of the smooth-talking cadence was Nick, without a doubt.

Nick and Britney? Together. In the chief's office. Behind closed doors. Lily's heart sank.

When the doorknob jiggled, she bunny-hopped backwards into the open broom closet across the hall before they caught her eavesdropping. Nibbling her thumbnail in the cramped space, her pulse pounded in her jugular over her panicky breaths, making it harder to hear their words. She hoped she didn't pass out in here. Wouldn't that be hell to explain?

She'd peeked between the crack and caught the backside of Britney dressed in thigh-high boots and a fur jacket, stuffing money her pocket. And Nick with red lipstick on his cheek. The rumors of Britney being a hooker were true!

No! This. Can. Not. Be. Happening. Her brain screamed, but nothing passed her lips except for hollow breaths.

She needed air.

Needed to get out of the closet.

Out of the building.

Out of town.

She loved Nick, but was too foolish and afraid to tell him. Now it was too late; he moved on.

Running out the back door, she thanked God she didn't collide into anyone.

Halfway home, operating on autopilot, heading in the direction of the blinding sun, she remembered her car parked in the lot behind the barbershop. She didn't realize the stream of tears until her cheeks were stinging from the cold.

"Pull yourself together," she urged, huffing and puffing white vapor clouds.

Once she barreled through the front door, she dove onto the bed, sobbing into the pillow until she was too exhausted to do anything but sleep off the heartbreak. She woke up with an emotional hangover at four in the afternoon of the same *craptastic* day.

With nothing left to lose, she turned on the laptop—a gift from Christmas past from the Secret Santa Society—and searched the web for New York City salons. Within an hour, she made a dozen phone calls and scored three interviews for tomorrow morning.

Now all she needed was an outfit other than her a velour tracksuit. As discouraging as shopping was, it might prove to be the distraction she needed to get her mind off Nick.

And Britney.

Britney and Nick.

The outfit Britney wore today was probably from the pole-dancer department of Violet's Valise. Right up Nick's slut-loving alley.

Lily didn't need exotic attire. Just something contemporary and preferably stylish. Something from Walmart could work. However, when she stepped out the front door, her station wagon wasn't there.

"Humph!" She smacked her forehead, remembering where she'd left it, then trekked downtown slipping along the sidewalk coated in black ice. The roads would be riskier to maneuver on bald tires. It wasn't worth it for a new clothes. Still, she needed to drive the car home tonight, or else she'd have to hike this route at dawn, plus a few miles further.

Pausing to catch her breath in front of Violet's window, the memory of Nick's hands all over her body put a cramp in her stomach.

"Oh, screw it." She twisted the brass doorknob, pushing her way through the magic portal, to the land of cutout lingerie. A wave of vanilla and baby powder enveloped her like a warm blanket.

It wasn't so bad in here.

In fact, it was quite lovely, and larger than she expected. Not entirely pornographic as she presumed. Maybe there was something here for her after all.

In addition to see-through baby-dolls, peek-aboo bras, caribou-trimmed teddies, and blinged-out thongs in the window, less-flashy ensembles were in the back.

She steered clear of a canoodling couple with their hands all over each other, wincing at their PDA, and redirected her attention to the wide selection of jewel-toned velour tracksuits hanging on a round rack. Had she known about this modest collection she would have shopped here a long time ago, except everything was out of her price range, including the items in the clearance section.

Just because she brought the credit card reserved for extreme emergencies, it didn't mean this was a carte blanche spending spree. Flipping price tags helped the decision-making process.

Considering the frosty weather conditions, low-heels were the best choice. Amongst the stilettos, she found one pair of flats in her hard-to-find size-six—black suede knee-high boots with laces up the back and ruffle trim—on sale half-price at four hundred dollars! She cringed, nearly choking on a mint.

The beautiful boots were so far out of her price range she should have dropped them and run for the door. But she took them anyway, carrying the big box in both arms as careful as if it were a baby.

Next, she found a hunter green knit dress that fit in her comfort zone on sale for a *mere* hundred-fifty bucks.

The purple curtains on the three dressing rooms against the back wall were closed. Lily peeked underneath to see if any were available.

Two sets of feet—small bare ones with French-manicured toenails and a pair of men's loafers—

occupied the one on the left. The newlyweds were in there, Lily presumed, imagining what they could be doing.

She skipped the vacant middle room and aimed for the one on the far right.

Unfortunately for her budget, everything fit perfect.

Posing in the three-way mirror, she noticed lines from her cotton panties. *Unacceptable.* There had to be a solution aside from wearing a thong.

She poked her head out the curtain, and beckoned the saleswoman. "Excuse me."

The elegant-looking lady with silver-streaked hair asked, "May I help you?—oh, hello, Lily. I didn't see you come in."

Feeling sheepish in strange new clothes, Lily smiled awkwardly at one of Sophia's friends. "Hi, Marie," she whispered, "I, uh, need something to go underneath."

"Hmm." Marie gave a liberal nod after a quick inspection. "It looks very good on you. However, it can look better. Wait—" She held up her palm and hurried away, returning with what looked like a piece of skimpy skin on a hanger—nude spandex with a lacey panel down the center. It was very pretty and looked impossible to put on. "It's a control slip. Built in wire-cups. Shapes your hips, tummy and tush all in one. Hides any lines. Give it a try." She left her alone to dress in private.

Stripping down to her boring hip-huggers, Lily didn't know which end to get into. Did it go over her head? Or was she supposed to step in it?

Over the head didn't work at all—it was like

jamming a ten-pound boloney in a five-pound bag. She tried the other method, wiggling her hips until the cool, stretchy material reached her boobs, and she could pull the straps over her shoulders. Smoothing out the painted-on fabric, she liked the way it felt on her body and under her hands.

Like a human sausage.

She struggled to reach the clasp between her shoulder blades, spinning in a circle, hoping the mirrors would be her guide. A dog had a better chance of catching its tail.

"Marie?" she sang over the heavy breathing from the couple two thin walls away. Lily peeked out and saw her at the register tending to customer, so she gave it another try and finally connected the two narrow tabs.

Aah. She silently applauded her solo-success, then wiped the perspiration from her hairline and studied her reflection. The dress would probably look better now, but after working up a sweat she was in no mood to try it again. *It fit without the slip, so it'll fit with it.*

The slip alone didn't look half-bad.

Hmm. If Nick could see her now, she'd make him regret hooking up with a skank like Britney.

Ugh! Thoughts of Nick and Britney had her seething. And to think, she went to the firehouse ready to pour out her soul to him.

Stupid. Stupid. Stupid.

Forgetting Nick Knight shouldn't be this painful. It was her own fault for being so weak. And it would never happen again. *I swear,* she promised her infinite reflection.

Now that she found what she was looking for, she could go home and wait for tomorrow to come, but first she had to get out of the slip. Another impossible feat.

"Um, Marie, would you mind helping m—?" Lily pushed aside the edge of the curtain and her heart stopped.

Chapter Ten

Nick stood ramrod straight on the other side of the flimsy dressing room curtain waiting for Lily to come out. Once it opened, his little soldier sprang to its fullest attention at the clear view of her hourglass figure.

If looks could kill, he'd be dead already. "What the hell are you doing here!" she growled through clenched teeth.

The eyeful of her nearly nude body scattered his thoughts, leaving him dumbstruck. "Geez!" slipped past his slack-jaw. Of course she had curves under those tracksuits, but he had no idea she was stacked right and tight, a well-proportioned powerhouse. *Good, God!*

She yanked the curtain closed, but the glorious vision was already branded in his brain. "Go away, Nick."

"I want to talk to you," he whispered rougher than he intended.

"Well, I don't want to talk to you." Her powdery voice radiated through the thin barrier.

The urge to rip the fabric off the rod crossed his mind, but he squashed the impulsive idea. Sure, approaching her on the sidewalk would have been a better idea than stalking her. But what he lacked in good sense, he made up with intrepid determination once he set his mind on the coveted prize. Inconvenient timing wasn't going to stop him. This game of cat and mouse was getting old.

Thinking of games, was it not but two weeks ago she'd told him flat-out how she *never* shopped in this sex-apparel store? Now, lo and behold, here she is, shopping—her least favorite activity, if he recalled correctly.

Lily peeked out with blazing eyes. "What are you still doing here?"

"What are you doing? Period." He rumbled low enough to avoid attracting the attention from the salesclerk, his mood growing more volatile with each passing nanosecond.

"I. Asked. You. First."

"Okay, fine. You're right. You asked first." He ran frustrated hands through his hair. "I saw you come in here. I wanted to talk to you so I followed you. Now, would you tell me just who the hell you're planning on wearing this get-up for?"

She jerked the curtain closed again.

"Lily, just come out so I can talk to you."

"I can't."

"Why not?"

"I can't get this thing off."

The salesclerk was with a customer. "Want me to help?"

She poked her head out. "Are you kidding?"

"I'm sorry about Thanksgiving." As soon as Nick took a step closer, she shut the curtain. "I never should have pressured you to talk. I'm a jerk."

Her fingers parted the curtain once more as she

leaned out to say, "You're right, you *are* a jerk."

Nick seized her hand so she couldn't disappear while he unloaded the weight in his heart. "I've missed you like crazy. You're all I think about. I'm sorry for everything. I can't pretend it doesn't bother me that we haven't figured out this thing between us. I know you feel something for me, too."

When Lily opened her mouth, he expected her to scream. The first tear fell; he caught it on his fingertip. "You're right. I do."

"I just need to know if there's someone else in the picture."

"Are you serious?" she squealed. A broken smile twisted her pretty lips as she dug her fingers painfully into his hand, inching her way out of the dressing room. "You have some nerve accusing me...after...after I saw you!"

"What are you talking about?"

"Oh, give me a break." She shoved his chest. "You're gonna make me spell it out? Okay. Fine. I. Saw. You. With. Britney," she hissed, smiting him with her laser vision. "I didn't think you were so hard-up you'd be willing to pay for it."

Stunned and confused by the accusation, he shrugged. "I don't understand. Pay for what?"

"Sex!" she shouted.

Two doors down, the noisy couple poked their heads out of the curtain with ruddy cheeks and ruffled hair.

"Don't worry—we're not talking about you." Nick pushed Lily into the dressing room, and she yanked him along, propelling his back to the mirrors. This infuriated woman giving him the evil eye was almost intimidating if she wasn't so damn adorable. "I didn't have sex with Britney."

"I saw the two of you. Together. In the chief's office. You paid her."

"Yeah. That's right. I did pay her. For *lunch*." He went on to explain the food delivery from the diner.

"Oh." Lily stepped back, a lovely shade of crimson spreading across her creamy exposed skin.

Nick stepped forward, swapping positions, pinning her in the corner. "So, you're jealous," he whispered. "Silly girl, thinking I want Britney, when it's you I've wanted all this time." He brushed tendrils away from her face. "I'm flattered."

"Well..." She refused to look up. "I-I..."

"You, what? Spit it out, sugar," he teased. There was no way she could conceal the glow of embarrassment. Afraid she'd start hyperventilating, he cut back his taunting before she passed out. "Are you trying to apologize? Because if that's the case, I accept, fully and completely."

"I-I..." She wet her lips and he took it as a yes.

He curled a finger under her chin and tilted her face, thrilled she didn't fight his tender kiss. But when he tasted her salty tears, he pulled back to swipe them from her cheeks with his thumbs. "You can't imagine how much I've missed you."

"I missed you, too." She panted the words like a drunken midnight confession and it was all he needed to hear.

He crushed his mouth to hers, while his hands encircling her ribs, trying not to squeeze too hard under the pressure of his greedy fingers. Her equally desperate kiss should have been proof enough. Still he couldn't resist asking the barrage of questions, only softer this time. "Who are you buying this for? Are you seeing someone else? Tell me and I'll stop."

"No. There's no one else. Only you."

He paused to study her eyes, seeking the truth. As hard as it was to imagine a catch like her staying single for too long, he believed her. "I need to see you." It was a plea more than a demand, and his groin strained painfully behind his zipper to prove it. "Will you go out with me tonight? We don't have to talk. I just wanna be with you. We can go for a drive. A walk. Get coffee. Or ice cream. Anything. Anything you want. I just wanna be near you."

"Ice cream?" She perked up.

"Is that a bad idea?" He winced, recalling her affliction for sweets and perfect teeth.

Her smile brightened. "Ice cream is never a bad idea."

"Okay. Ice cream it is," he said, even though it was freezing outside.

After unfastening the slip, he stepped out of the dressing room while she changed.

She emerged a few minutes later wearing a coy smile.

He took the merchandise from her hands. "Let me buy it for you."

"You don't have to."

"I want to." He pulled out a wad of cash at the register. "See anything else you like?"

"Nick, you really don't have to— Okay, fine," she exhaled. "Since I know you're wondering, it's for a job interview tomorrow—well, three interviews. In Manhattan. I need to make a decent impression."

"You look great in whatever you wear." *And even better without—*

"Thanks. But you're not hiring me."

"Which votive would you like?" The sales clerk indicated to the stubby little candles in colors that matched their fragrant names: Gingerbread Boyfriend, Lavender Fields Forever, French-Kiss Vanilla, and Forever and Evergreen. "It's free." The sign on the counter read: *COMPLIMENTARY GIFT WITH YOUR PURCHASE.*

"No, thanks." Lily waved them away.

"Go on, take the candle." Nick sniffed the green one. It smelled just like a Christmas tree.

"Nah, it's okay. I don't do candles."

"What do you mean? Girls love candles. That's why they're giving them away."

"Not me."

"What about on birthday cakes? Don't tell me you don't do birthdays either?"

Lily frowned. "Birthday candles are for children who believe wishes come true."

"But wishes can come true." Nick was determined to prove it.

"You don't have to burn it," the saleswoman said. "Use it to scent your lingerie drawer. Or for decoration."

"Oh, fine. I'll take that." Lily pointed to the one in Nick's hand. "Thank you," she said to the clerk. Then her eyes drifted dreamily at Nick. "Thank you, too."

He carried the packages and offered to drive her

to her car, which she accepted without a cross-examination.

"What's that?" Lily indicated the big red bag between them on the bench seat.

Making room for her, he quickly stuffed it into the back with the gear he'd forgotten to remove. "That's just the Santa suit."

"Not *the* Santa suit?"

"Yep."

"Can I see it?"

"On Christmas." He threw the truck in Park next to her orange station wagon. "If you're a good girl."

"Oh, I'm good, all right." She giggled and he caught a naughty gleam in her forgiving eyes.

"How about I follow you home—that is, if you still wanna to go out..." He escorted her to the car, nervous, like it was his first time asking a girl on a date.

"Sure."

He opened the door, but she hesitated, with eyes big and bright like two glittery stars. The white vapor of their breath mingled in air. Thank God the tears were gone. He hated seeing her cry. And felt worse being the cause of it.

"Nick, I..." she started, but her quick pink tongue moistened her bottom lip, beckoning his mouth to come closer and he couldn't resist the kiss.

Warm.

Deep.

Long.

A steamy slice of heaven in her lips lingered after they pulled themselves apart.

"Wow." She swiped her mouth dry with the back

of her hand.

"Get in the car before you freeze."

He followed her home with his windows open so the icy air could clear his head. When they pulled into her driveway, he parked behind her, waiting with the engine running.

She ambled to the driver's window. "Would you like to, um, come inside?"

"Uhh, sure!" Her invitation was the right step in a better direction. A million times better than last time he brought her home.

Nick followed Lily up three concrete steps and she hip-checked the front door, grumbling, "It sticks sometimes. Just needs a little shove."

"Let me try." He jiggled the key in the lock and leaned his weight against the warped wood until it finally opened.

She flicked a wall switch and a floor lamp in the corner set the small space aglow. Tiny and tidy as it may be, it was easy to figure out why she wanted to sell it. Bringing this time capsule of eclectic eras up to today's standards would take a lot of money. Dark wood paneling covered the living room walls and worn ornamental rugs hid most of the dull linoleum floor. Like his place, it would be easier to tear down than fix up.

"Sorry it's so cold in here. The heater is behaving badly." She breezed through the living room to the kitchen on the other side of the half-wall.

Cold was an understatement. He pushed on the front door to make sure it wasn't the source of the major draft. A quick glance at the windows and he spotted the culprit across the room; the kitchen window over the sink was opened an inch and arctic air rattled the curtain like a ghost.

"Do you want something?" She indicated to a selection of large gift baskets on the floor lined up along the kitchen wall. "They're Christmas gifts from clients. Take whatever you want."

He *wanted* Lily but knew that wasn't what she meant.

Staring through the cellophane, he studied the innards of the array of baskets: cheese and crackers, pastas and sauces, smoked sausages, herbal teas, flavored coffees and creamers, candies, cookies, gourmet hot chocolates, baking items, and other treats. There was even a basket of assorted soup.

She flicked on the oven and pulled down the door. "It'll warm up in a minute."

"It could be a whole helluva lot warmer in here if you kept that window shut."

"Yeah, I would if I could. That's as far as I can get it. I usually stuff it with a dish towel to cut the breeze."

"You do know that using the oven to heat your house is a fire hazard."

"I only do it when it's really cold. Just to take out the chill."

If she did this with a firefighter around, he worried what she does while he's gone. "I'll check the chimney. Then you can use the fireplace." And he could scratch the last name off his list.

"Don't bother. I won't use it anyway."

"It's safer than using your oven." He reached over the sink and applied gentle pressure on the corners of the brittle wood, closing it all but a few millimeters. Nailing it shut might help, but the glass may shatter in the process.

She snapped the dial to the Off position. "Better?"

"Much."

"Let me know if you go numb, I'll get you a blanket."

"I have snow gear in the car."

"And don't forget the Santa suit."

"Definitely not. Can't forget that," Nick sniggered, dreading having to wear it in a few weeks.

On the topic of Christmas, her home wasn't decorated like the rest of the neighborhood, outside or inside. Not a wreath. Or a bow. Or a piece of tinsel. Or a string of lights. Nothing. Except for the little spruce leaning in the dark corner of the living room.

"Nice tree."

"It was free. One of Bob's clients runs the lot."

"You gotta water it otherwise it'll dry out." Another potential hazard once she put lights on it.

"I haven't gotten around to it." She turned up the antiquated thermostat in the hallway and the heat came on with a painful groan. "How's your bungalow? Still coming along okay?"

"Not really. It looks like I might be a permanent resident at the firehouse until I can fix a bunch of issues. I won't be able to do any major work until spring."

"Hmm. Well...I've got a room for rent. It's not much. I can show it to you if you're interested."

Toes curled inside his boots and his fingers

tingled with excited energy. "Actually, yeah, why not?"

He followed her down the short hall to view the piece of real estate that—unbeknownst to her—he was in the process of buying. It didn't take long to put two-and-two together, realizing it was *her* advertisement from the community bulletin board he washed with his jeans.

"I should have rented it a while ago. I was hoping I wouldn't have to. It's a tiny bedroom. Used to be my parents'. I'll move out the junk to make room for you if you want it."

As long as the bed was big enough to stretch out in, he didn't care about the piles of things, stacks of cardboard boxes, or the viva-la-seventies décor. "This'll work just fine."

"Really? You're serious?"

"Absolutely." He nodded, doing his best to forget about any ulterior motives. "Are meals included?"

"I don't cook—but I can make sandwiches!"

"Well, I guess you're in luck, because I *can* cook. I'll have to teach you."

"I didn't even tell you how much the rent is."

"Trust me, you won't blow my budget."

"I guess that means you're gonna stay the night then? I'll just take the stuff off the bed for you—"

"Leave it for now. I can stay on the couch."

"I'll give you the grand tour." On the way to the kitchen, they stood in the hallway and she pointed to the four doors within arm's reach. "Bathroom. My room. Linen closet. Cellar."

"You're sure you really wanna sell it?"

Lily curled up in a wooden chair at the little round kitchen table, smoothing her palms over the faded floral tablecloth and shrugged.

Nick sat across from her, anxious to know more.

"It doesn't really matter. I can't afford to keep it. If I could, I'd never consider selling it. But it's all for the best, I guess. With the money, I can get a decent apartment far from here. And I'll never have to run into Britney again."

"Didn't you hear—Britney's spending the winter down south."

"Hallelujah." Lily clasped her hands to heaven. "What else did she say?"

Nick hesitated, like mentally preparing to rip off a bandage, before spitting out the rest. "Well, she talked about her brother. And mentioned something about her mother's ring."

"She told you I stole it, didn't she?" Lily scowled and shot out of the chair. Filled the teakettle with tap water and slammed it on the stovetop. While it heated, she rummaged through the kitchen drawers, smacking each one closed with a vengeance, until she pulled out a silver key and handed it to Nick without explanation; no doubt the spare to the front door.

He slipped it into his back pocket.

"Nobody stole anything," she ranted, chest heaving. "As far as I know, Mark's mother gave it to him to sell, which is just what he did. I told Britney a dozen times, I never even saw the ring. Not unless it was ever on their mother's hand. Their parents had been divorced since Mark was in elementary school. The ring obviously didn't matter much to him or his mom. I don't know why it matters so much to her. At least she has her parents. I don't have anyone. I don't have anything—my mom hocked all her jewelry to keep up with the mortgage payments before she over extended the credit cards she opened in *my* name. That's why I'm in such a financial mess."

When she poured steaming water into a chipped coffee mug with shaky hands, Nick got up and nudged her aside. "Let me do that."

"That's why I need to get outta this town," she murmured. "And start over somewhere else where people don't know my business..."

He followed Lily to the living room with two steaming cups of cocoa and sat beside her on the tattered burgundy loveseat. There was a terrible draft on this side of the house blowing on his ankles through thermal socks and insulated work boots.

"If you rearrange the room so the couch isn't blocking the fireplace, it wouldn't be so chilly against your back. The wind coming down the flue is as bad as the kitchen window."

"I just wear a lot of layers."

"Now that you have a roommate, you can't let me freeze. We'll have to do something as a temporary fix."

"I don't even know where to start."

"Relax. I'll handle it."

"I need the rent money for bills. I can't invest in repairs."

"Well, you're looking at a pretty handy guy." And in the spirit of being *handy*, he set his cup on the table, then rubbed the soft fabric covering her thigh.

She stared pensively into space. "I-I have to tell you something. Getting back to what we were talking about…on Thanksgiving."

He halted her before she could start, not wanting to backtrack to him being a hard-ass that night. "No, let's just *fuggetaboutit*."

"I can't. Please, let me just say it, and then if you don't like it you can leave."

"Okay, fine."

"There's another reason why Britney hates me. The *real* reason…You see, Mark and I-I didn't know it, not until the doctors told me, but at the time of the accident…I, um, I was a few weeks pregnant. And I lost the baby."

Wincing with her words, he felt her pain like a kidney punch. "God, Lily, I'm sorry."

"We were always really careful. But one time the condom broke, and that's all it took. The thing that still bothers me is, even if I hadn't lost it, I don't know if I would've wanted to have it on my own. His family would've wanted it—to have a living piece of Mark. I don't think I would've had the heart to give it up. And I was in no position to raise a child—God, look at me now, I can hardly take care of myself. Could you imagine if I had a baby?"

Yes. "And Britney blames you? That doesn't make sense."

Lily choked back a sob of fresh tears. "She thinks I…that I terminated it on purpose."

So, this is what she'd been too afraid to tell him. Had he known, he never would have pushed her. "Aww, Lil." He wrapped both arms around her, pulling her into his lap. In the dull light, he saw the agony in her eyes and lines of torment tugging her frown. "Please don't cry."

She covered her face with her hands like a child. "You must think I'm a terrible person."

"No. Not at all." He collected her slender wrists with one hand to keep her from hiding. "Your history doesn't change how I feel about you."

A fleeting smile flickered before she buried her head in the crook of his neck.

"Lily, look at me." She needed to know the gravity of his emotions. "You believe me, dontcha?"

"Yes. I believe you, but…"

"But what?" He read the deliberation in her eyes. Her words came too slow for his brain's warp-speed.

"Remember when you asked how I felt about children?"

"Yeah."

"Honestly, I don't know. Remembering how I felt at the time…it was terrible. I hoped by now—that I'm older, still none the wiser—I'd feel better."

"Lily, you lost the baby. It's not your fault."

"I know." She swiped an escaped tear.

"You can't beat yourself up forever. Do you believe things happen for a reason?"

"I guess so."

"Well, I know so. Take it from an old dog like me—meeting you was no random thing. I really believe God put me in Scenic View to find you."

He held her for a while, enjoying the quiet peace. By the time he realized Lily had nodded off in his arms, he was halfway there himself, leaning back with one foot dangling over the armrest and the other on the floor. On her stomach, sleeping between his thighs, she used his torso as a pillow. He could get used to this position, and a few others, but he'd reserve those passionate thoughts for another time.

Sleeping with her, *literally*, was good enough for now.

****

"What time is it?" Lily awoke with a groan.

It couldn't be morning yet. The windows were dark, except for the sliver of streetlight between the curtains. Straightening her crooked neck to see the clock on her nightstand, she realized she wasn't in her bedroom. And her lumpy mattress was a rock-hard wall of manly chest and abs clad in soft flannel.

That meant everything wasn't just a fantastic dream!

She pinched herself to be sure she was awake.

She was.

Slowly, she peeled off Nick, not wanting to wake him. He looked so serene despite slouching in the corner of the loveseat. She cupped his warm cheek, sliding her palm over the rough stubbly surface. Running fingers through his dense hair was tempting, but she settled on brushing the dark fringe off his forehead.

Last night had been an overwhelming relief, realizing his feelings ran as deep as hers. No more denying the electric charge between them. The chemical reaction. The *zing*.

After revealing all the things torturing her soul for so long without generating the negative side effects she'd feared, she never wanted to let him go.

Howling wind and delicate tinkling against the

glass inspired her to peek outside. Snow, and lots of it, covered the world as far as she could see. There was something magical about the first snowfall of the season.

And there was something magical about waking up to Nick. The drafty old house didn't feel so cold with him around.

She needed this kind of companionship. She needed *him*. Now that she had him where she wanted him she could rest easy. Snuggling against his chest, she drifted back to sleep.

"Lily?"

Lost in a dream, Nick's tender voice roused her while his fingers played with her hair.

"Lily. Lil. Wake up."

"What? Why?" She sat upright, stretching, as he rolled from under her.

"I need to go out for a while."

Fear tightened in her belly. "Is there a fire?"

"Don't worry, sugar. It's just snowing. I gotta take the plow out." He grabbed his leather jacket from the coat tree.

"Can't it wait until sunup?"

"Accumulation makes it harder. I gotta start now. People need to go to work in the morning." He kissed her forehead and covered her with the afghan, leaving her with a Terminator impression, "*I'll be back*."

Chapter Eleven

He must have finally lost his *friggin* mind, voluntarily leaving the warmth of Lily's embrace to freeze his *cojones* off. With zero visibility, driving was a nightmare. The roads were impassable for anyone without a plow.

Toggling the joystick on the control pad, Nick dropped the blade and angled it toward the right, making a first pass down Sunflower Summit to Main Street. Then he turned around and repeated the process until it was clear.

The mechanical task cleared his mind as well. He could only focus on this one thing right now, otherwise he might take off the bumper of a car. What were these people thinking—parking in the street during a blizzard when they had driveways.

The more important question was—what was Lily thinking when she asked him to move in? Hopefully her offer wasn't based on the heat of an emotional moment.

Just what the hell was he thinking when he agreed?

Fending off his sexual frustration living under the same roof was gonna be impossible. The challenge had him adjusting his jeans. He cracked the windows to cool his raging hormones. The frenzy between his head, heart, and hardness had him driving in circles.

His heart wanted to go straight to Lily's, while his head nudged him toward the firehouse to check-in with Maresca. But in the end, the painful strain in his pants won.

He plowed a path to the marina, parked in his usual *meditation* corner, and took care of some *personal business*.

Now that the dirty deed was done, and the snow had tapered off, he could head home for a little while.

Before putting the truck in Reverse, his cell phone jangled the old-fashioned ringtone that belonged to one person. "Hey, Tristan. What's up?" Nick braced himself, as no good news ever came from his best buddy at such an early hour.

"Hey, bro. Did I wake you?"

"I'm up to my nuts in snow. How're things in Star Harbor?"

"We got a dusting, that's it. So, how'ya been? I haven't talked to you in a while." Tristan sucked in a breath like he was smoking a cigarette—something he only did under major stress.

"You're not calling me at six a.m. to tell me you miss me, are you? Everything all right?"

An audible exhale vibrated over the line. "Stacy moved out. I got home from work an hour ago and all her stuff's gone."

Nick winced. Tristan and his wife's marital problems weren't anything new. "She'll come back. She always does. Right?"

"I hope so—but not for my sake. I'm sick of her

shit. I'm calling a divorce attorney. The only reason I want her to come home is because of the baby."

"Wait—she didn't take Nicole?"

"Nope. She left my sister in charge. I'm gonna call my in-laws. They're flying in from London for Christmas, maybe they can change their plans and come sooner. Her daycare's only Monday through Friday. I'll find someone to watch her on nights and weekends."

"If there's anything I can do, let me know. She's my goddaughter. I love her like she's my own, you know that."

"You're a little too far away right now." Tristan's breathing dragged. "I have no choice but to rely on my sister."

"Are you sure that's a good idea?"

"She may be a wildcat, but she'd never hurt Nicole." Tristan cleared his throat. "Umm, while we're on the topic of Claudine—do you know she's looking for you?"

Nick figured as much seeing how she'd been calling three times daily for the past couple of weeks, never leaving a message. "I hope you didn't tell her where I am."

"I would never, bro. But maybe you could just talk to her—?"

"No. *Friggin.* Way."

"Come on, will ya, she's my sister. Do it for me."

Nick had the sick recollection of those same words nearly twenty years ago. *"Come on, she's my sister, just do it for me. You don't have to marry her, just take her on one date."* That one date had led to a wedding and the single biggest mistake of his life. Groaning before responding, he wanted to avoid any misunderstanding. "We. Are. Divorced. There is nothing left to say."

"I get where you're coming from. But you know how relentless she can be. I'm sure she'll find you sooner or later. She's pretty resourceful."

"Do you know what she wants?"

"Probably one of your pep talks. Husband-number-three tossed her out, which is why she's been staying in my guest room. She said you don't answer her calls. Maybe you should, so she doesn't show up on your doorstep."

After Tristan hung up, Nick mulled over the information on the slow ride home. The last thing he needed was his ex-wife appearing in Scenic View to stir the *shit-pot*.

He didn't want to think of Claudine.

Lily was all he needed. She made him tipsy without drinking a single drop.

When he got home, he brought in his duffel bag, a big flashlight, and a facemask from the backseat, wanting to check the chimney before lighting it up.

She wasn't on the couch, so she was probably in her bed, unless she'd ventured to the train station on foot since her car was boxed in the driveway. He wouldn't put it past her. However, her blue puffy coat was still hanging on the coat tree.

First things first, he made a pit stop in the bathroom after hours of drinking coffee. It was colder in here than the rest of the house because a piece of plywood was all that covered the small broken window.

Next, he moved the couch so he could reach the firebox. He'd call a professional to do a complete sweep, but it looked good enough for now. During his coffee stops at the mini-mart, he'd picked up a dozen fire-starting logs—enough to keep warm for the weekend until he could get a couple cords of wood. Wouldn't she be surprised to wake up in the morning to heat for a change?

Outside her bedroom, he whispered, "Lily—can I come in?" Her door was ajar and he peeked inside.

In the bit of gray morning light peeking between the parted curtains, it looked like the usual teenage-girl's bedroom, complete with stuffed animals cluttering every corner, posters of cats and dogs dressed like people, and flowery border-paper.

Asleep beneath a bundle of blankets, with a teddy bear nuzzled under her chin, she looked too comfortable to disturb.

"Mmm?" She stirred, lifting her head. "Nick?" she said dreamily.

"Hey, sugar." He braced his hands on the sides of the doorway in an effort to keep a safe distance. "I didn't mean to wake you."

"How are the roads?"

"Better than they were. But it's still flurrying. It'll have to be done again."

"Now?"

"No..." He released one hand to cover a yawn. His other hand slid off the doorframe as he dared to inch into her private domain until he was standing at the foot of her bed. "Later. I'm gonna recuperate on the couch for a while."

"You can lie with me," she offered, making

room. She slid against the wall, pushing the teddy bear onto the floor.

Straining to bend with his jutting erection, he retrieved her doll and tossed it at the foot of the bed.

"I, uh, I really need to get some rest before I go back out there. I don't think I can fall asleep without…" *Without seducing you first.* "I don't think I can fall asleep with the light in this room."

She reached up and closed the curtains, solving the problem. "How's that—better?"

"Thanks, but I need *real* sleep. Alone sleep. No offense. Being next to you will keep me up." *In more ways than one.*

Her smile slipped away. "Are you sure?"

He bent and kissed her forehead. If he lingered too long, he'd take her up on the offer and wind up taking things too far—or worse, venting about his ex-wife. "I'm sure."

****

Lily woke up sweating, feeling like she'd been sleeping on the sun. "Oh, no!"

She kicked off the blankets and ran to the kitchen to make sure she didn't leave the oven on all night as usual.

It was off, but the fireplace was on.

Nick reorganized living room, moving the couch to its original position as it had been during her childhood, where she could stand on the cushions and see out the window.

Watching him sleeping there now reeled her back in time.

The image of Daddy in that same spot, napping in front of a roaring fire, was a bittersweet memory

129

she'd thought was lost in the crowded void of her mind. Her heart hurt at the evoked emotions.

But things were better now that Nick was here.

While her *roommate* slept, she cleared away the miscellaneous items stored in the spare room. *Nick's room.*

She found his red-checkered flannel shirt in the laundry room and sniffed the collar. It was a shame to wash it being how it smelled just like him. Curiosity had her slipping into it, just to see what it felt like over her t-shirt. *How would it feel with nothing else?*

Maybe he'd let her borrow it sometime.

The telephone rang and she muted it, refusing to answer the collection agencies' calls. They'd get their money as soon as she closed on the sale.

With a foot of snow on the ground, and more to come, there was no way she could go anywhere, never mind New York City. Especially with Nick's big truck blocking her car. It was a good enough excuse to cancel the job interviews. Sure, working at a prestigious salon might be the way to a happily ever after, but after last night, everything changed.

She had a boyfriend and a roommate wrapped up in one hot package, spread-eagle and snoring peacefully on the couch. His tight blue jeans accentuated his not-so-little soldier, making her practical panties moist.

Go on. Touch it. You know you want to.

Her palm hovered above his zipper in a stealthy attempt to size him up. Based on the plump bump between the inseam and button, he was longer than her pinkie and thumb at their furthest points. It was tough to determine the girth without wrapping her fingers around it. A sex pistol so big, backed by the magnitude of his body, could do some unintentional damage for sure. Maybe it wouldn't hurt very much if she were on top where she'd be in control.

Undersexed, she was overanalyzing everything.

Needing to get her mind out of his pants, she quickly dressed in warm clothes and headed outside where the arctic blast soothed her feral fever. Icy flakes clung to her lashes before her body heat melted them like tears.

She clomped through the snowdrift to find the shovel behind the house.

An hour later, she was numb and exhausted from clearing the heavy, wet snow from the front steps and making a narrow path to get to their vehicles.

"Whew."

She paused to catch her breath beside the buried mailbox, sweating despite the cold. The lopsided little house looked postcard-perfect beneath a pillow of snow. More than it ever did. Maybe it had something to do with Nick's face peering through the frost-covered living room window, waving her inside.

He leaned out the front door. "Lily! I'll handle that. It's freezing. Get in here."

She propped the shovel against the house and stomped the snow off her boots. "I can't b-b-believe it's still c-c-coming down."

"You're letting out the heat." Nick pulled her inside and shut the door.

He began undressing her, beginning with the snowy hat, hanging it on the coat tree. Then the knit gloves. He unwound the scarf. Unzipped her coat and she shook it off shoulders, shivering uncontrollably. When he got down on his knees to untie her frozen laces, she held onto the top of his shaggy head to keep from falling over, as he pulled off each boot.

"What's on under here?" He tugged her pant leg.

"Thermals."

"Just checking." He loosened the dangling drawstring and hiked down the damp layer.

"And under here?" He grabbed the hem of her sweatshirt.

"Thermal undershirt." She lifted her arms so he could remove the bulky layer over her head, revealing the puckered-gray fabric that matched the bottoms, making her look like a skinny elephant.

Then, without warning, he pressed her against the wall, kissing her hard on the mouth. Clinging to his sleeves as if her life depended upon it, she couldn't protest even if she wanted to. He was strong and gentle at the same time, holding her in place, molding her body to his. She was melting all over again, with his hard, thick shaft pressed against her stomach.

This is it!

She wanted this. Wanted him. Even if it meant taking a little pain in the process. He was worth it.

When he lifted her off the floor, cupping her bottom, she wrapped her legs around his waist and anchored her arms behind his neck. With their lips locked, he carried her to her room.

In between breaths and kisses, he mumbled, "You worked hard today. Maybe you wanna go back to bed for a little while."

Here it is.

Her stomach clenched. The moment she'd been fantasizing about. His ginormous joystick. *How am I going to handle it? Will it fit? Will it hurt?* Should she avoid the pain and just offer to go down on him before agreeing to go all the way?

He dropped her backwards on the mattress with a bounce. "There's cocoa for you." He pointed to the mug on the nightstand. "I thought you could use it."

"Thanks." He'd already warmed her enough, but to be polite, she sipped it anyway.

"I'll see you in a little while." He backed out of her room.

"What—why? You're going out to plow? Now?" She glanced at the clock. It was after three. The snow stopped, and the fading sky was a dirty gray outside her window.

"One of the town's plows blew an engine."

"I don't understand what that's got to do with you. You work for the fire department." She was just getting used to having him around and they were already on opposite schedules. Her hot and bothered libido wasn't letting him go without a fight.

"We're in a state of emergency. I'll be back in a few hours."

"Would you lie with me for a little while first?"

"I really oughta go...I wanna start before it gets dark." He held the top of the doorframe, lingering like he didn't want to leave. The hem of his shirt lifted, and Lily's eyes followed the faint furry arrow that disappeared in the waistband of his jeans. "The sooner I go, the sooner I come back. Then I can lie with you all night long."

"Okay. Sure…later."

"Come on. Don't be upset."

"I'm not. I just…" *I just want you to make love to me.* "I was just hoping for a moment…"

"All right. Five minutes. Then I have to go before the chief sends the dogs to find me."

Chapter Twelve

Back in the saddle again, clearing a fresh batch of snow, Nick battled his guilty conscience for not telling Lily about his phone call with Tristan. Now that she was finally letting go of her inhibitions, he didn't want any more setbacks.

After making a second pass down Main Street, he stopped at the firehouse and poked his head in Maresca's office. "How's it going, Chief?"

"Hey, Nick, come on in. I'm just going through some of these letters to Santa. Where ya been?" He eyed Nick curiously over a pile of papers.

"Where else?" Nick nodded toward the snow-covered window. "Plowing."

"Better make sure you get some rest then."

"I did."

"Oh, really? I didn't see you in the bunkroom."

"Yeah, well, that's because I found a place yesterday."

"What'd ya get—an apartment?"

"A room in a house."

Maresca shot him a quizzical look. "Mind telling me where?"

There was no sense delaying the inevitable. Nick would have to deal with the repercussions once her inner circle knew he was living under her roof. "Um, over at Lily's."

"Lily Lane?" Maresca straightened his spine. "Is that so?"

"Yep." He folded a piece of gum into his mouth, giving him something to do with his loose lips besides saying too much. "She's got a spare room." He glossed over the dirty details.

"Ah…that's right." Maresca nodded, sitting back, drumming his hands on the armrest of his chair, pivoting from side-to-side. "Let me ask you a question—and I know it's none of my business—but is this just a *convenient* living arrangement? Or is there something going on between you two?"

Nick hesitated, uncertain what the better answer would be. "What do you mean?"

"What do you *think* I mean?"

"I like her, if that's what you're asking…" A calming wave of relief washed over him. "I like her a whole lot—a whole *helluva* lot." He couldn't think of enough ways to say it without admitting he was totally head-over-heels in-love with her. But she ought to be the first person to hear it before he announced it to the world.

"That's good to know, because I'd hate to think a decent guy like you would mess around with a good girl like her. She doesn't need any more heartache in her life. She's had plenty."

"She told me."

"You better not lead her on." Maresca's warning was as threatening as any father figure.

"That's not part of my plan."

"What *is* your plan then—if you don't mind me asking, man-to-man."

"She's good for me. And I'll be good to her, don't worry. I'd ask her to marry me right now if I thought she'd say yes. I've never met anyone like her."

"Hmm… If that's the case, then I oughta give you something." He dug a piece of paper from the drawer.

"What's this?"

Maresca jutted his chin. "Read it."

Nick mumbled, "*Emotionally available*. What's that supposed to mean? '*Nick*.' Nick who?"

"Who do you think?"

"I dunno. You tell me."

"It's *Lily's* letter to Santa."

"How do you know? There's no name."

"I know her handwriting, I've been reading them for years. Think you can handle it?"

"Absolutely."

"I had a feeling you could. When I saw you at Brawny's together, I had the inkling something might be up. It was strange to see your name on the letter, but I guess the girl knows what she wants."

He folded the small note in half and tucked it in his pocket. By the time he got home, the fire was out and the house was freezing again.

"Hey, you," her groggy voice whispered from the couch. "What time is it?"

He hated that he woke her, because now he'd have to try extra hard not to make love to her. Try even harder not to tell her about his latest and greatest super Santa secret.

"A little after one. What happened—why'd you let the fire go out?"

137

"I don't trust it burning while I'm asleep."

"It won't hurt you if you care for it properly. People have done it for centuries."

He lit another log. It wasn't as romantic as a real stack of firewood, but it was good enough for now.

"Better than TV, dontcha think?" He joined her on the couch and pulled her head against his chest. "Tomorrow we'll get that tree into some water."

"The stand and decorations are in the cellar. Let's get 'em now!"

It was the last thing he wanted to do, but her hopeful smile was so bright he couldn't refuse. "Show me the way."

He went first down the concrete stairs while she pointed the flashlight, holding the belt loop on his jeans. The stink of mothballs and mildew worked wonders on killing his sex-drive.

"Over there." Lily pointed the light at a brown heap that looked like a cardboard snowman slumping in the corner. "I haven't opened these since Mom died."

Nick hoped there was something worth salvaging in the corroded, moldy boxes.

While he set up the tree, she examined the contents on the kitchen table.

"Aww. I made this in kindergarten." It was a decayed candy cane decorated with a pipe cleaner resembling a reindeer.

"You know what...let's put these outside. You'll get new decorations." He took the box away before she found something she really didn't want—like roaches.

"Wait." She stuck her hand inside and pulled out

pieces that looked like a cracked crystal snowflake on a silver ribbon. "Aww. This was my mother's. It's ruined. Everything is ruined."

He probed around to find something worth saving, but the sentimental objects were destroyed, dangerous shards of glass tinkled at the bottom.

"Sorry, sugar, but you can't keep this stuff." He wedged himself between her and the shattered memories. After he discovered a rodent's nest, he did the thing she didn't have the heart to do—close the boxes and toss them in the trash. Then he washed his hands and grabbed her in a tight hug.

"You'll get new things. I promise."

"Yeah, sure. I know." Droplets sparkled on her lashes.

The oncoming tears stabbed his heart, so he pulled out a wad of cash and dropped a hundred dollar bill on the table. Then another. And another... "I don't think we talked about your rate. Tell me when to stop..."

"My *rate*? What? Stop it!" She slapped his fist full of money. "What are you doing? Put that away."

"You asked me to be your roommate, right?"

"I did."

"Do you still want me here?"

"I do."

"Well, I don't expect to stay for free. And I'm gonna need some comforts of home—like a properly decorated Christmas tree." Forking over more bills, he added, "How am I supposed to get into character for my big debut? We need lights. Tinsel. A wreath. Some fake snow. That green stuff to hang around. Stockings—one for you, one for me. What else? Oh, yeah, candy canes, of course."

"Huh?" She glanced at him as if she missed half of what he said, shaking her head in disbelief. "This is a thousand bucks. You carry this much cash in your pocket?"

"I pulled some emergency money from the ATM," he lied. There was about ten thousand stashed in his glove compartment. "How long does a grand get me?"

"I dunno—ten weeks."

"You're asking a hundred dollars a week to rent that room?"

"Too much?" She bit her lip and wrung her fingers as if she'd never done this kind of negotiation before. No wonder she was selling her house for such a steal.

"Not at all."

"I can't cook, but I can do laundry."

"You mean wash it, or wear it?" he teased, tugging on the collar of his flannel shirt, which looked perfect on her.

Color bloomed in her cheeks. "Sorry. I was chilly. You can have it back." She started unbuttoning it.

"No." He didn't want her taking it off, unless it meant seeing her naked. "You can wear it. But you can't keep it. It's my favorite. How about we share it?"

She looked confused if not a little relieved. "Share a shirt? How?"

"I'll tell you all about. In bed. I'm exhausted. I need to lie down before I fall down." He led her to his room where he stretched out on the mattress and patted the empty spot beside him.

"I...uh...I dunno..." She shrank against the wall.

"Come on, Lily, don't get shy on me now. I'm not talking about going all the way. But I'm ready to figure out this chemistry between us. The living arrangement. That shirt..." He got up and closed the gap between them. "We're better under one blanket together than alone in two separate rooms, dontcha think?" He took her by the hand and she didn't resist. "We'll even keep our clothes on, I promise."

She sat on the opposite end of the bed, hugging her knees like a shield against her chest.

"You don't have to be nervous."

She furrowed her brow. "I'm not."

"Are you sure you want me here? Because if you changed your mind, I can go—no hard feelings," he lied. "I don't wanna make you uncomfortable in your own home."

"Of course I want you here. It's just...I wasn't expecting to sleep in the same bed."

"I get it, and I'm willing to wait, but doesn't mean I'm not thinking about it twenty-four seven."

She gathered the shirt collar protectively and released an uneasy giggle.

He grabbed the fabric from her fingers, pulled her closer until they were nose to nose. Lust swelled in her eyes with pupils like big black dots.

She *was* ready, he could tell.

Now if he could convince her of it...

"So, tell me. What's it gonna be—freeze alone in your room, or stay warm with me tonight?"

Chapter Thirteen

Lily's head spun from his invitation. It sounded more erotic than a platonic nap. Especially with the devious gleam in those dark eyes staring into her soul. Nick bit his bottom lip, which prevented his crooked smile from spreading too wide.

"*Well*?" His warm breath tickled her cheek.

Of course, she'd choose being with him over anything else in the world. But didn't want to seem overzealous, afraid of looking like a whore. She couldn't hide her burning desire if she tired.

"I know you wanna." He leaned back on the stack of pillows, patting the place beside him. "I'm just tired, and I want you here. You're gonna make me beg, huh?"

"You don't have to beg. It's just…I don't want you to think I'm…easy."

"Oh, sugar, you're anything but easy. That's what I like about you. Make me work for what I want. Now, come on, and get next to me." He lifted the blanket.

She swallowed the lump in her throat and surrendered. "All right."

"Good girl. Get comfortable." He eased her back. "See. Not so bad, now, is it?"

"No. Not at all."

"You sure?" Propped on his elbow, he looked down on her, nose to nose.

Her heart was in a frenzy, and her body was ready to burst into flames. "I'm sure."

"God. You are so beautiful." He caressed her cheek. "I'm not just saying that because I wanna do things to you like you can't even imagine."

Hot memories of sizing up his manliness while he slept flashed in her mind. "Nick, I...I want to. You know I do. But I don't want to rush into anything."

"Yeah, yeah, I know. But you can't control everything—especially destiny. You have to let go eventually. I think now's a good time to start. There are plenty of things we can do with our clothes on."

His kiss was tender and soft, as their tongues swirled together. It was a good thing she was on her back, because the lightheadedness came on hard and fast as the blood drained away. "Mmm."

"Are you okay?"

She struggled to open her heavy lids. "Oh, yeah. Why?"

"You made a noise...I didn't hurt you, did I?"

"I'm fine. Really." His big body leaning on her ribcage didn't bother her. She pushed herself up to reach his lips, but he resisted.

"On second thought, maybe we're better off on the couch after all. Or in the kitchen. Or we maybe we could, uhh, make a snowman, or something."

"In the middle of the night?" She chuckled at his sudden change of heart.

A grimace crossed his face as he adjusted the crotch of his jeans. "I won't be able to control myself if we keep doin' this."

"Oh, sure you can. I don't want you to stop kissing me now. Or maybe we can do *other* stuff…like you said."

"I can't…I just…" He rubbed a hand down his face and shook his head. "I dunno what I'm doin' anymore."

"You don't have to do *anything*." She massaged his calf, creeping up his thigh. "Just sit back, relax, and let me do the work."

He jumped off the bed, scowling. "What are you talking about?"

"What do you think?" She waggled her eyebrows at his inseam.

"I have an idea—let's bake cookies."

"Cookies?" *Is that code for blowjob?*

"Sure. I think it's time for a cooking lesson. We'll indulge in, uh, *sex-education* another time. Don't take it personally."

He kissed her forehead and nudged her toward the kitchen, where he tore open the gift basket of baking supplies.

"You're right. Let's pace ourselves. Now fetch me some butter, woman." He gave her a playful slap on the bottom. "And take out the eggs." He winked, and followed it with a sincere, "Please, if you don't mind, love."

His authoritative tone was a turn-on; she did as she was told, concealing a secret smile.

So much for the lesson. Nick did all the work while she watched, daydreaming as she stared at his tush in those well-worn jeans like he was born wearing them.

A short while later he pulled a fragrant tray from the oven.

"Smells yummy." Her mouth salivated, but not for the chocolate chip cookies as much as the man that made them.

When they finished devouring warm cookies dunked in icy cold milk, Lily rolled up her sleeves, ready to clean.

Nick scooted her aside. "That's okay. I'll handle it."

"No, no, no." She dragged him to the couch. "You cooked. I'll clean. Roommates share responsibilities."

"Don't give me that *roommate* nonsense." He tugged her down beside him before she could get away.

"Okay. Fine." She didn't want to wash dishes now anyway.

He curled his arm around her and dropped long leisurely kisses along the side of her neck. "I know this might sound like a line, but I've never felt like this before. Ever. About anyone."

"Me, too. I just don't want to do anything we'll regret."

Pulling her hair at the crown, he tilted her head and searched her face. The firelight set off an ethereal glow in his eyes. His lips touched hers, making her melt into him like an ice cream cone in the sun. When his tongue skimmed along her bottom lip inviting her mouth to open, she complied, waiting for it, wanting more of it. More of him.

"I know you wanna wait. And I'm willing to. At least I'm trying to. But I believe the only thing we'd ever regret is not making love."

The dynamic words pricked her nerves. He was right. What if he wrapped himself around a pole next time he went out in this weather? No doubt, she'd regret letting this moment slip away.

Then his cell phone went off, shattering the mood. Drunk-dialing or emergencies only came at this time of night. He ignored it, while Lily cringed, recognizing the moody ringtone after hearing it enough times.

"Just answer it already! Find out what she wants and be done with it."

"Hell, no!" He left it at that as he always did, which satisfied Lily since she didn't want his ex-wife's interference anyway.

She straddled his lap, seeking his full attention, finding his full arousal.

"What are you doin'?"

"You're right. I don't want to live to regret anything." In her heart of hearts she would never regret making love to this man.

"You know what would be fun?"

"You don't *seriously* want to make a snowman, do you?"

"Not really," he laughed. "I was thinking you could put on the outfit you got." He wore a wicked grin with a naughty twinkle in his eyes.

Heat rose in her cheeks. "Is that so?" She couldn't hold back the smile or stop the challenging words from falling off her lips. "And what are you gonna do for me?"

He cocked an inquisitive eyebrow. "What do you want?"

"How about you put on the Santa suit?"

"Nice try, but no way."

"Come on, please, do it for me."

"Santa is an old fat guy. What's sexy about that?"

She rubbed her flannel-clad breasts against his chest. "Maybe I have a Santa fetish."

"Maybe you just want me to feel stupid."

"I'll do it for you, if you do it for me—"

He rolled her off his lap and dashed outside.

A moment later, he returned with a red sack over his shoulder.

On the way to their respective bedrooms, he gave her tush a love-tap. "Get dressed, sugar. Santa Claus is coming to town early."

Lily shook the contents of the Violet's Valise shopping bag onto her bed. The votive tumbled onto the floor and she picked it up. One whiff of the heady balsam fragrance had her pulse pounding as the memory of Nick in the dressing room flooded her mind...The desperation in his eyes. The apology. The kiss. And to think, she nearly gave up on him.

"Ready or not..." Nick warned as she stuffed herself into the slip, forgoing the impossible clasp. She tugged the dress over her head as he knocked. "Here I come!"

The door swung open.

Standing in the hall was a perfect-looking Santa Claus—belly, beard, and all. He adjusted the silver belt buckle and smoothed down the fur trim. "Do I look okay?" Wearing white gloves, he scratched the silver wig under the cap.

Lily bit back a giggle. "I'm sorry. I'm not

laughing at you. I'm just—wow! You look like the real deal. The quintessential St. Nick."

His twinkling eyes scanned her body with a devilish grin that looked nothing like any Santa-smile she'd ever seen. "Ha ha ha. But this Santa's no saint."

"That's not how it goes. Say it right."

"Don't hold your breath."

"Aww, come on." She enticed him with a little shimmy in her shoulders. "You oughta practice."

He shook his head like a stubborn child. "Nope."

"I won't let you unwrap your present if you don't."

"I'll do it anyway." He inched closer, caught her around the waist, and pulled her against his soft foam belly. "You're one *naughty* little girl. Teasing Santa with these tight clothes and your wicked mouth. Making Santa behave badly. You're a little *ho-ho-ho,* aren't you?" He scooped her up as he sat on the bed, placing her on his lap.

"Is that all padding in there?" She poked the spongy area where his rock-hard abs ought to be. "And this beard. It's so soft. It tickles." She swatted it away from her neckline.

"Dontcha believe in Santa?" He raised his naturally dark eyebrows—the only telltale sign of Nick underneath, aside from the excited *elf* in his pocket, poking her hip.

"Of course I do."

"Good. Because only children who believe will *receive*." His sultry act was nothing like any department store Santa Claus. "So, what do you want for Christmas, little girl?" His words were slow and deliberate, expectant and knowing, and she felt herself go wet between her thighs at the hot innuendo in her ear.

"You really want to know?"

He nodded. His hand rubbed her knee with a cool satin glove. "Tell Santa everything."

"Well, *Santa*, what I'd really like is a man."

"Interesting…tell Santa more about this *man*."

"Does Santa always talk in the third person?"

"Yes, Santa does, always. That's just the way Santa operates."

"Well…" She bit her lip in a quick deliberation. "I'd like him to be nice."

"You know what they say…nice guys finish last. They let the woman finish *first*. Have you been a good girl this year?" His finger tickled the back of her knee.

Lily covered her mouth to hide a wanton whimper.

"Let it out. Santa wants to hear you."

"Well, *Santa*…" She sucked in a breath. "I'm trying—but it's hard your hand between my thighs."

"It's been a long, cold night. Santa needs to get warm. But if you don't like it…"

"No." She clamped her knees together, trapping him. "I like it where it is."

"That makes Santa very, very happy." His other hand rubbed the small of her back in a figure eight. "Tell Santa more about this man you want."

"I'd like him to be smart and sweet. Sincere. Kind. And gentle."

"Are you sure you don't want a woman instead? That might be fun for you. And me—since Santa sees you when you're sleeping…"

"No, thanks. I definitely want a man. Good-looking. Strong. And sexy." Her cheeks burned as she described her ideal man to his disguised face.

"Okay," Santa growled. "Now we're getting somewhere."

"Tall. Dark. Mature. Emotionally available."

"*Emotionally available*? Hmm." He made the thoughtful noise.

"And he has to have a sense of humor. Be a good kisser…" Her voice dropped.

"An emotionally available, mature, good kisser, huh? Something like this?" He leaned in and planted fur-lined lips on her neck, just below her earlobe as his hand slipped up the hem of her dress.

"Mmm…yes, Nick…just like that."

"Call me Santa…" he panted, as he shifted their position so her back was against the mattress.

"No, that's silly."

"Just do it for me." It was Nick's voice, his eyes, mouth, touch, but all she could see was Santa, and it took all her willpower not to laugh aloud.

"Okay, fine." She sighed. "Oh, Santa, baby…"

From head to heels and back again, St. Nick dashed kisses over her exposed skin, tickling a trail with the beard. He slipped off the dress and body slimmer with an expert touch, as if he was peeling a human banana.

Gloved hands persuaded her body into easy submission as she stretched out on the bed beneath a red blur and a flurry of white. Christmas was coming early, and she was getting everything she wanted for the first time in a long, long time.

"Tell me when to stop."

"Don't." She wriggled at the tickling-teasing sensation of satin fingers swirling her belly button. "Don't. Ever. Stop."

He tugged off the beard. Pulled off the gloves. His warm palms encircled her waist as he kissed her belly. Then caressed her naked thighs, pushing her knees apart. His finger slipped under her panties then penetrated her honey pot.

"God, you're so wet," he whispered in amazement.

"Oh, yes," she hissed with magnificent anticipation as he worked off her underwear one-handed.

Then, like an incessant ice pick in her brain, that damn doom-and-gloom tune destroyed her good mood. Unlike Nick, she couldn't ignore Claudine's interference any more. She slammed her knees together and pushed him away.

"Get off me and just answer the phone already!"

Chapter Fourteen

The last person in the world Nick wanted to talk to was Claudine. Especially with Lily ready, willing, and naked beneath him.

"She *obviously* wants to talk to you." Lily rolled off the bed.

He collapsed in her warm space and curled an arm around her fragrant pillow. "I don't want to get mixed up in her problems."

She flicked on the light. Nick couldn't take his eyes off her curvaceous bottom marked with Dimples of Venus above each perfect cheek.

"You can't ignore her forever. What if it's important?"

Lily grabbed a long, pink bathrobe from the hook beside her bedroom door, next to the incremental tick marks on the jamb that started low until it reached her current height. A visual reminder of their wide age-gap. Guilt bloomed in his belly. But her bouncing breasts confirmed she was all woman, old enough for him in every way imaginable.

"*Well?*" she asked.

"Well, what?" Too busy fantasizing about her figure, he'd missed the question.

Raising her brows, she glared at him, looking

crazy-sexy as hell, with tangled hair, and her face flushed from foreplay. "What if Claudine has something important to tell you?"

"She can leave a message like everyone else."

"Maybe she's not over you."

"Maybe you're right, but it's a little too late for that."

She marched out, mumbling, "Well, the heart wants what the heart wants."

"It's not her heart that wants me!"

Nick crossed the hall to redress in a pair of black sweatpants and a black thermal shirt from his duffle bag, then met Lily in the kitchen.

"Whenever her heart gets broken she comes looking for me to fix it. Make her feel good again. Build her up. Let her know she deserves better. I can't be her go-to guy anymore. Getting divorced was supposed to be the end of the relationship. Just because I didn't sever ties with her brother, and she and I share a godchild, doesn't mean we'd get back together one day. No. Way."

"Did you ever tell her that? Some people need it spelled out."

"Of course, I told her. Maybe it wasn't clear enough when I said 'Stay the hell away from me you crazy bitch!' Maybe she didn't believe me. She came looking for me after her second divorce, and I patched her up and sent her back into the world. She's been married to number three for a few years. Took him long enough to realize she's insane. I didn't expect she'd hunt me down here."

Lily's eyes expanded twice their size. "*Here*?"

"I dunno if she's serious." He omitted the details

of his ex-wife's historic harassments. "But that's what Tristan said."

"So, what are you gonna do?"

"I dunno. What can I do? What would you do?"

"Hmm, what would I do if some lost-and-found lover of mine kept coming back for me? I dunno. If I still loved him, I guess I'd rethink my feelings. What's that saying: 'If you love someone set them free, if they come back to you, they're yours forever, if they don't, hunt 'em down and kill 'em.'" Lily smirked.

"That's not funny."

"What's she like anyway?"

"Bleached-blonde, blue eyes, tall. She looks a lot like Britney actually."

Lily's face fell. "Oh."

"But I've always had a soft spot for redheads." He pulled her by the lapels. "When I look at you, I see a future I never imagined. A future I always hoped for, but thought was for other people. Not guys like me."

"You really like me *that* much?" An authentic smile spread to her glittery eyes like the first day he saw her in the liquor store.

"Yes," he whispered with a kiss.

"Well, next time she calls, answer it, and let her know you've met someone new." She yawned. "I have to get up for work in the morning."

"Get to bed. I'm gonna check the fire first."

"Don't take all night." She walked past her door and into Nick's bedroom.

After putting on a new log, he sat on the couch and watched the blaze. He loved a roaring fire when it was under control.

He loved Lily more. She wasn't like other women. She was something special and deserved nothing but the best. His best.

But he couldn't be his best when his ex-wife still managed to bring out his worst.

He stretched out on the couch, giving Lily a chance to fall asleep alone, as he'd have a hard time controlling his craving once he got under the covers with her. Sex wasn't the way to prove his feelings, especially when Claudine was on both their minds. He wanted to make love when they could concentrate on nothing but each other.

Sometime during the night, he crawled into his bed, thrilled to find a warm bundle of Lily to curl up with on a cold night.

In the morning, the alarm clock's incessant beeping jolted him to awareness, but he turned it off before she woke, wanting to laze little longer with her nestled against his chest.

Eventually, she showed some sign of life.

"What time is it?" She sat upright, scratching her wild hair.

He loved how she looked with sleep still fresh on her face. "Ten."

"I thought I set the alarm for seven. I have to be at the shop at nine."

"I'm pretty sure everything's closed because of the snow."

"If it's open, then I have to go to work. How else can I afford to live in this lap of luxury?"

"Why dontcha just live in the luxury of my lap for a few more minutes?"

He maneuvered her into a spooning arrangement with his arousal throbbing in his sweatpants against the curve of her bottom. It was an impossible position to maintain without causing him agony, so he flipped her around as if her supine position would feel any better beneath him.

Kissing her from above, his hands moved below the blanket, hoping it would be enough to convince her to stay in bed all day.

She swatted him away, covering her mouth with her hands in playful protest. "Get away. I don't want to share my morning dragon breath with you."

"If you can't share it with me, then who can you share it with?" He suckled her neck instead.

"You're crazy."

"You're right. I'm crazy about you. I keep telling you that. When are you gonna believe me?"

Her house phone jangled, wrecking the moment.

"Probably bill collectors," she grumbled, grabbing the handset off the nightstand to read the caller ID. "No—wait. It's Bob. Good morning," she sang. Giving Nick wide eyes, she shushed him with her finger to her lips. "I think Sophia's right, you should stay home today. But, sure, if you want, I'll go with you."

"Tell him I'll drive."

****

Not even half-a-day after their love-fest weekend ended, and Lily missed Nick like mad.

Although Bob knew about her feelings for the firefighter, she wasn't ready to give out the dirty details about their living arrangement just yet. The last thing she wanted was for Sophia to find out.

As expected, the shop was void of customers. Neighboring business owners who made it down Main Street were the only people to walk in, talking about the Nor'easter.

However, all Lily could think about was Nick. She might explode from keeping him all to herself, locked in her head. She couldn't wait to get home, back to bed.

To kill time, Bob sat in his empty barber chair watching ESPN.

Lily stood by the door, admiring the world from behind the frosty glass, drawing hearts in the fog.

The sidewalks were a mess. Ankle-deep snow turned to slush under the afternoon sun. The roads were narrow yet passable. Snowdrifts the size of miniature mountains would last for days, if not weeks, so the mayor decided to cart as much as possible to the marina and dump it in the Long Island Sound.

Maybe it was the positive effects of falling in love, but aside from being slippery as all hell, life looked as glorious as a glitter-coated Christmas card. For the first time in a while, she was actually looking forward to the holiday now that she wouldn't be alone.

Things with Nick felt so good. So right. It was hard to believe it could be true. He was an all-around amazing guy. Any girl would be lucky to catch his eye.

No wonder his ex-wife wouldn't let go.

Lily had faith that his former relationship was a non-issue. Nevertheless, the more she thought about it, the more it bothered her. And the more it bothered her, the harder her blood boiled until it pounded in her ears.

To cool off, she grabbed her coat and ventured outside, expending some frustrated energy, pacing the clean portion of the sidewalk.

She trusted Nick. There was no reason to doubt him. Everyone has skeletons. Baggage. Issues. Remembering how empathic he'd been when she shared hers, she needed to extend the same respect.

With each step, she inched closer to Farley's pharmacy next door, until she was standing inside.

After last night, so close to taking things to a deeper level, she realized they hadn't even talked about protection. It wasn't foolproof, as she'd learned the hard way. Still, it was a better idea to be prepared.

The array of condoms hung on end-cap in front of the register. She skimmed the selection from a safe distance to avoid looking obvious. She never bought them before. When she was with Mark, she didn't have to. He handled it.

Itchy fingers were anxious to grab a box so she could get the hell out of here before someone noticed her. There were so many to choose from, she spot-checked the labels for comparison. *For Her Pleasure* was a popular theme. No doubt, Nick would supply all the pleasure she needed.

No matter how nonchalant she was, Lily couldn't avoid the clerk's watchful eye a few feet away. She grabbed the smallest box and camouflaged it with some decoy items—cinnamon gum, a word-search puzzle book, and a dark-chocolate bar.

The clerk gave Lily a curious look that prompted

her to conjure a half-lie on the spot. "They're for a friend." She forked over a hundred-dollar bill and snatched the change and the paper bag before rushing back to the shop to hide her purchase in her backpack.

Within the hour, Sophia magically appeared after catching a ride into town with the son of one of the Ladies'. She sat behind the counter, snapping her gum, flipping through a magazine, while Bob concentrated on the television.

"You know, we could have done this from home." Sophia scowled.

"Oh, *shaddup* already." He waved his wife away. "You didn't have to come."

"I need to make sure you're okay. My crazy husband *had* to come to work today. Tell me again, how you got here without your car?"

"Same as you—one of Chief Maresca's guys," Bob snapped. "Now be quiet so I can watch TV."

"Ooh, really. Let me guess which one," Sophia said smugly just as the telephone rang. "Hell-oo?" She sweetened her tone for the caller. "Is that so?" After a long stretch of silence, she hung up, cutting her eyes at Lily. "What's wrong with you?"

"Headache," Lily lied.

"So, is that why you went to the drug store? For aspirin?" Sophia glared.

Answerless, Lily returned the elder woman's angry stare.

"A whore buys condoms, not a lady!"

Damn the clerk with the big mouth. "It's none of your business. Besides, it's not for me. It's for a friend."

"What *friend*? Who—that man? Rick? Vick? *Whateverhisnameis*? A decent man takes a lady on a respectable date, not straight to bed. Am I right, Bob?"

Lily was mortified.

"Leave her alone," Bob said. "It's not our business."

"But she already agreed to meet my nephew. He'll be here in a few weeks."

"I didn't agree to anything. You just presumed I needed a blind date."

"That's because Bruno's a great catch. Nick's no good for you. He's a fireman. God, what would your mother say?"

"Enough already!" Lily grabbed her coat and bag.

"Where are you going?" Bob shouted over the shrill.

"Home!"

****

While Lily was at work, Nick stopped at the *Everyday's Christmas* shop and bought enough decorations to cover the small tree from the skirt to the star. He spent the rest of the day at the firehouse taking care of business.

Before it got dark, he swung by Bob's to see if they were ready to go. As soon as he stepped in the door, his cell phone droned his ex-wife's notorious ringtone; he cringed and dumped the call to voicemail. "I'm looking for Lily."

Sophia stopped filing her nails and gave him a dirty look. "Oh, really?" She wobbled around the counter wagging her finger. "I don't know what's going on between the two of you, but whatever it is, I don't like it. My nephew is *perfect* for her. He could be her golden ticket to a good life. He's *my* first choice—"

"Then I'm glad it's not *your* choice."

"When she meets him, and he sweeps her off her feet, don't say I didn't warn you."

The door jingled just in time.

"Hello, dear," Sophia sang. "I was just telling Lily's *friend* that she went home already."

Bob stopped short as if he slammed into an invisible wall. Two Styrofoam cups slipped from his fingers and hit the linoleum floor.

"I'll get the mop." Sophia waddled to the backroom.

As Nick walked out, Bob grabbed his elbow.

"Hey, I don't know what my wife may have said, but I know her opinions can be a little critical. Personally, I think you're a decent guy. Why don't you take Lily out to dinner, or a movie, some place nice, you know? This way she can tell Sophia. And Sophia will get off her back. Then everyone'll be happy."

He felt a little better with Bob's support.

With all the inference from Sophia and Claudine, Nick was lucky Lily was still interested. This relationship was already like walking on black ice; he didn't need these opposing forces working any harder against his sincere effort.

Before he walked in the house, he remembered to put his phone on vibrate.

"God, I'm so glad you're home. What a terrible day!" With a freshly scrubbed faced and damp hair, wearing purple fleece pajamas, she looked like a teenager ready for a sleepover party. "I'm sorry I didn't call to tell you I left early. I just needed to cool off, so I walked."

Playing dumb, he asked, "Why, something happen at the shop?"

Lily tossed a tiny box; he caught it and read the label. *Condoms, huh?* Nick cleared his throat and shifted his stance to adjust the excitement in his pants.

Sophia's onslaught made better sense now, and Bob's recommendation rang in his head like a fire alarm.

"Get dressed, sugar, I'm taking you out tonight."

Chapter Fifteen

After all these years of enjoying the Christmas splendor from the outside, Lily finally saw the inside of the Scenic View Inn.

It was more spectacular than she imagined with the twenty-foot tree in the center of the lobby, adorned with nautical-themed ornaments. Hundreds of crystal snowflakes dangled from the stained-glass cathedral ceiling. Oversized poinsettias flanked the mahogany reception counter. Corner to corner, green garland, red bows, and tiny white lights covered every wall and window.

The place was a whimsical vision, professionally decorated by *Everyday's Christmas* as per the little posted sign.

It truly was the best place for a *real* first date.

Nick's jeans and flannel shirt didn't meet the dress code, so the hostess recommended the lounge instead. Lily preferred the dark, cozy ambience anyway.

It was too cold for the skimpy green dress tonight, so she wore a black tracksuit. Next time he wanted to take her out, he needed to give her more than five seconds to get ready. If she had it her way, she'd be home, in pajamas, under the covers, curled in his arms.

At a table for two, Nick held Lily's hands, running his thumb over her knuckles, not taking his eyes off hers. "So, what about dessert?"

After devouring a basket of fresh rosemary bread, followed by the chateaubriand with mushrooms and roasted potatoes, Lily couldn't eat another bite.

"Nothing for me."

"Just order something. Anything. It's our first official date. Let's go all the way. How about ice cream?" Candlelight shimmered in Nick's hopeful eyes.

"Fine."

"Bring us something special," he said to the waitress.

"So…what else did Sophia say?" she probed. He was such a vault, downplaying the details regarding the conversation that sparked the urgency for this unscheduled date.

"Not much." He gave a slight shrug then sipped his seltzer.

"Well, I'll be sure to tell her all about it tomorrow morning." She twirled the ice in her cherry soda with the straw.

"Make sure you show her the receipt if she wants proof." He winked. "But the Barbieris are right—you deserve to be treated like a lady."

A salad bowl-sized sundae arrived with two long-handled spoons.

"A lady doesn't need twelve scoops of ice cream."

Nick dug in first. "Don't worry, I'll help you."

"My hero," Lily teased, shoveling a fluffy

mound whipped cream covered with rainbow sprinkles into her mouth.

The sundae didn't stand a chance. They annihilated it while talking about Nick's past and their future.

"So, your grandmother raised you?"

"I never knew my dad. I don't even think my mother knew him beyond that one night. She tried doing it as a single parent, but it was a struggle. Eventually, she met some guy. They fell in love and wanted to get married, start a life together—a life that didn't include kids. I guess that's why I want my own. I think I'd be a great father."

Lily nodded. "I think so, too."

"Really? You do?"

"Of course. You're a great...guy. I'm sure you'd be an excellent dad."

"What about a husband? That's an important component to get from point A to point B, dontcha think?"

"We've only known each other two months. Aren't we moving a little fast?"

"Maybe. But it feels right, doesn't it?"

"Yes, but..."

"But, what? I'm thirty-six and all grown up," he said with a dab of strawberry ice cream on his chin. "I'm ready now. For marriage. Kids. The works. I'm just waiting on you." He took another mouthful and stared at her with earnest eyes, as if he was waiting for an answer to an unasked question.

It was impossible to hide the smirk no matter how hard she tried. "Nick."

"I know. I know. You're not sure about kids."

"Never mind what I said before." Lily waved the words away. "I'd love to make a baby with you…one day."

"I'm not even going to ask if you're sure. I'm gonna take your word for it."

Lily envisioned their best qualities combined to make a new little person. There was no doubt Nick was the only man for her. "I like you better than most people I've known my whole life." The words fell from of her lips as natural as rain.

"I know exactly how you feel."

"Where's your grandmother now?"

The light in his bright eyes dimmed. "She passed away when I was in the Marines."

"I'm sorry." She bit back a tear for the broken-hearted little boy inside this virile man.

"Grandma Dorothy would have loved you."

"I wish I could have met her."

"She was a spunky little lady. And a great cook. I know all her recipes." Nick tapped his finger against his skull.

"You oughta write them down."

"You're right. I will. Someday."

"So, how'd you meet Tristan?"

"He lived next door to Grandma."

"You've been best friends for a long time."

"More like brothers. He's a cop in Star Harbor. He and I do carpentry on the side. As kids, we constructed this incredible fort in his backyard from stuff we stole from the neighborhood. I helped him build the nursery for his daughter. It came out amazing. I got pictures..." He pulled out his Smartphone and swiped the screen. "Wait I missed a bunch of calls. Speaking of Tristan..." He stood, staring at the device like it was a lifeline. "It might be something important. I'll be right back."

"I'm going to use the ladies' room." Lily went with him to the lobby before heading in separate directions after a parting kiss.

The bathroom was the size of her whole bungalow and elegant like the lobby with the same touch of holiday flair. A marble partition separated the toilet stalls from the sinks and mirrors. Soft piped-in music played a piano rendition of Jingle Bells. There was even a sofa and a baby changing station.

She aimed for the vanity counter to check her reflection for any remnants of hot fudge.

Despite her best effort to mind her business, it was impossible to tune out the calamity from one of the stalls—a bawling baby, and a mother begging it to stop.

"I'll find it. Or I'll get you a new one. Just stop crying already! Please!" The mother's frustration echoed in the confined space. Then the stall door flung open, and she rushed out of the restroom with the child in her arms.

Lily stepped out a moment later.

On the way to the lounge, she spied a tattered scrap of pink fabric and picked it up—no doubt, that baby's blanket. The woman was nowhere in sight, so Lily gave it to an employee in case someone came looking for it.

By the time she got back to the table, Nick was already there with a pensive look on his pale face. "Everything okay?"

167

"Not really."

****

As soon as Lily mentioned the baby and mother in the bathroom, Nick knew exactly who it was. He called Tristan on the spot to give him the update. Then he grabbed her arm after slapping a couple of hundred dollar bills on the table.

"Where'd you see 'em?" His eyes scanned every face.

"In the bathroom. But they left ahead of me. I don't know which way they went."

"Where was the blanket?"

"There." She pointed to the wall, near a coffee table with a plate of complimentary cookies, beside a heavy leather chair.

There was no other evidence that Nicole and Claudine might be here. Just Lily's observation of two platinum blondes and a pink baby blanket. "Are you sure the blanket had lambs on it?"

"Pretty sure. It was square. About this big." She gestured the shape and size. "The girl was young…a toddler. I don't know. I'm not really a good guesser when it comes to age."

"You're awesome." He kissed her head. "It's gotta be them."

"I don't understand…" Lily followed him to the hotel manager's office as he explained the details of a probable kidnapping.

Then Nick phoned Chief Maresca. "My buddy Tristan is gonna call you. Can you give him a contact person at the police department? We think his sister snatched his daughter, and she may have come here looking for me. My ex is bipolar, but I can't imagine her hurting the child. Then again, I'd rather be safe than sorry."

"If I knew...I would have done something..." Lily was nearly in tears.

He hugged her, trying to get her to calm down before she freaked him out even more. "Relax. I'll find her. Everything's going to be fine. Don't worry." He hoped he was right. "Go find the blanket."

The manager checked the records, but no one named Claudine was registered. Nick didn't know her new married name, so he asked to see the list of guests. "Stacy Casanova! She probably swiped the credit card from Tristan's wife."

"Room 429," said the manager.

On the way to the elevator, Nick met Lily in the lobby. "Yep. That's Nicole's." He smelled the blanket for memory's sake, praying silently that his ex-wife hadn't completely lost her mind to pull such a stunt. "Stay down here. Wait for the chief. I don't need you in the middle of this."

"But..." Lily's eyes were bright with fear as the elevators closed.

Of all the stupid, careless, selfish things Claudine has ever done, taking off with Nicole tops them all. When he found the room, he pressed his ear to the door before knocking. "Room service."

No one answered.

He thought about calling her cell phone but didn't want to do anything that might make matters worse.

Suddenly, his phone vibrated, and for once he was glad it was Claudine. "Hello?" He stepped to the end of the hallway, keeping his eye on room 429.

"Hi!" She sounded shocked. "I can't believe you answered. It's so good to hear your voice."

Nick choked back the bile. "Yeah, yours too. How ya been? Long time, no see."

"Too long. But I have a surprise for you."

"You know how much I love your surprises." Nick squeezed his hand into a tight fist, tempted to punch a hole in nearest wall.

"I'm getting divorced. Again. Isn't that...terrible." Claudine started weeping. "I screwed up another one, Nick. What's wrong with me?"

Everything. "Maybe it's not you," he lied. "Maybe it's the men you pick."

"I picked you. I should have never left."

With nothing better to say, he rattled a string of clichés. "Well, what's done is done. One door closes, another opens. All you can do is move forward from here. The best is yet to come. Hey, is that Nicole I hear in the background. How is that little angel?"

"Yep. That's our precious, little goddaughter." Claudine perked up and started speed-talking. "She's doing great. She misses you."

"She told you that?"

"Well, I can just tell."

"You always were the perceptive one."

"I am. I think I would have made a great mother..."

"Probably." Strobe lights out the window caught his attention. Five cop cars parked along Main Street with the sirens off, cherries and berries on. "So, whatcha doin'?" He hated pretending everything was normal.

"I'm on a mini-vacation."

"With Nicole? Sounds like fun. I talked to Tristan a few minutes ago. He told me about Stacy. He really appreciates your help."

"Is that what my brother said?" She sounded nervous, as she should.

Lying came easier with each word. "Oh, yeah. He's thrilled. So, where ya staying?"

"Well..." Claudine exhaled an uneasy laugh. "I'm actually at the Scenic View Inn."

"Isn't that something! I'm in Scenic View, too. Got transferred here a few months ago."

"Yeah, I know. That's why I came. To find you—surprise."

"You're always full of surprises." He faked a laugh through clenched teeth.

"So, you're not mad?"

"Why would I be mad?" Several reasons popped in his mind—harassment, stalking, kidnapping...

The elevator door opened and six cops filed out.

Nick signaled as they cautiously approached room 429. He pointed to the cell phone against his ear, then toward the door, and gave a thumbs-up, while listening to his ex-wife's teary meltdown.

"I just miss you so much. No one understands me like you. Maybe we can try again. It's like I can't breathe without you..."

"Take it easy, okay? Everything'll be all right. Why don't you and Nicole meet me in the restaurant? I can be there in five minutes."

Four minutes later, the cops cuffed Claudine in the hallway, her face pinned to the carpet, thrashing and screaming like a banshee, threatening to kill everyone in sight.

Nick grabbed his godchild and escaped in the elevator.

The moment the doors slid open, Lily was right there waiting. "What happened?"

"They arrested Claudine. Nicole seems all right, thank God." The child yawned, barely able to lift her head off Nick's shoulder.

The sergeant on the scene offered to send an officer over later to take the report and deliver the child's belongings once the investigation was complete.

"Come on." Lily nudged. "Let's get her to bed."

Chapter Sixteen

Despite the sub-degree temperature, Lily power walked to work feeling a whole lot better than she did after last night's fiasco with Nick's ex-wife.

The date was great.

Rescuing the child was even better.

The uncertainty in between had Lily's nerves in knots. She'd almost called in sick today, wanting to be home to help him with Nicole.

But he had things under control, so she went a little late.

Besides, she wanted to tell her bosses all about the good parts of the date to get Sophia off her case—but the woman wasn't even there.

Bob avoided any deep conversation, lost in his own thoughts. Eventually, he explained how his wife had gone away for a few days, on the first flight this morning to Florida, to watch the grandkids while his daughter and her husband hashed out the details of their divorce.

Between Nick's friend and the Barbieri's daughter, it seemed everyone one was getting divorced these days.

Lily hugged Bob, a quick, tight squeeze around his mid-section.

"I needed that." He sighed with a strained smile.

Bob was such a good man. A good boss. Father. Husband. Friend. Lily was lucky to have him in her life. And she was lucky to have found a man of her own who compared.

Nick should be here soon to pick her up, so she gathered her things but felt guilty leaving Bob alone tonight.

"Do you want to grab some dinner?"

"Just you and me? Or your *roommate*, too?" He gave her a curious look.

"Thanks for not judging me. Sophia makes me feel like I'm doing something wrong because I like him. And renting the spare room helps with the bills."

"Don't mind her. She means well. But she's a control freak. Hopefully you won't turn into one after you have a family of your own."

"We went on a date last night—dinner at the Scenic View Inn." She left out all the other details, figuring Bob had enough on his mind, and the story about the kidnapping would eventually make it down the grapevine.

"Fancy schmancy. Did he pay?" Bob joked with a broken smile that didn't reach his eyes.

"Of course." Lily sighed. "I really hope everything works out for your daughter and the kids."

"Yeah, me too. Children need two parents. I know that if your father were still alive, your mother wouldn't have..." He shook his head and made the sign of the cross. "I mean, what I'm saying is...your father kept her grounded. They were good for each other. She never got over the loss. That's the saddest part, because she had to take care of you." He gasped as he preached, struggling with the poignant words. "I always keep you in my prayers, Lily. In here…" He pointed to his heart, then groaned and clutched his chest.

She nibbled a fingernail expecting him to finish his sentence, but something wasn't right. "Bob? You okay?"

He folded to the floor.

"Bob!" Paralyzed by fear, the nanoseconds passed. "What do I do? What do I do?" She was petrified to put her knowledge into action.

She stuck her head out the door, shouting to anyone on the sidewalk. "Help! Call 911!" she shrieked.

Then she rushed to Bob.

On her knees, she smacked his plump, pallid cheeks. "Bob! Bob, can you hear me!?" she panted, expecting an answer.

There was no sign of breathing. "No. No. No!"

She aligned her palms to the center of his chest and started compressions, afraid she was hurting him more than helping. Her arms were tired after two minutes, but she kept going.

The door flung open and a variety of feet circled her.

"Back off everyone!" Nick took over, kneeling beside. "I got it from here."

Too shocked for tears or words, she simply watched him work until the EMTs showed up with the right equipment to kick-start Bob's heart.

"Clear!" Then after a long hush, "He's breathing!" They whisked Bob away on the gurney, and the crowd dispersed.

"Take a deep breath." Nick rubbed her back as she sat hunched over in the barber chair with her head in her hands. "He oughta be fine."

No amount of oxygen would shake this icky feeling.

"I'll take you to the hospital."

"Yeah, um, okay. I should, uh…call Sophia."

"Relax. I'll handle it."

Lily slipped on her coat with his help, and he carried her backpack slung over his shoulder. He took the keys from her shaking fingers and locked the shop, while she held Nicole's tiny hand.

On phantom feet, she followed him to his truck. He belted the little girl in the backseat while Lily climbed into the passenger side.

"Bob nearly died." Her eyes felt wet, and her hands were still trembling. "Even though I knew what to do, I was, like, frozen. But then, I dunno what happened. I just did it. Like you taught me. And to think I almost didn't come to work today."

"Lucky you did."

Lily snorted. "Luckier you showed up."

His warm hand squeezed her fingers. "You kept his heart pumping. If he were there for two minutes without blood to the brain, he'd be worse off than a few broken ribs. You did all the right things. You saved Bob."

She drew a shaky break and nodded, refusing to release his hand.

"Lily…about last night…after we just had a great weekend, and an amazing date, my ex comes to town and wrecks everything."

"Don't be silly. It's not your fault. I'm glad Nicole is all right. Why don't you drop me at the hospital, and you can take her home."

They glanced at the child smiling in the backseat, oblivious to the drama.

"Like the safety seat? It's a loaner from the police department. The officer brought it over last night."

"When's her dad coming?"

"I told Tristan not to rush since she's safe. I should have asked you first if it's okay she stays another night. Maybe two."

"Of course it's okay."

"It'll be good practice for us." Nick winked with a smile, then put the truck in Drive.

When they arrived at the hospital, Lily's head was still spinning, so Nick went to speak with the doctors, while she stayed in the lobby with the child napping in the crook of her arm.

She struggled to stay awake, focusing on the big clock over the silver ER doors, unable to stop the constant yawning.

Finally, her vision grew blurry so she rested her eyes…

Then a firm hand shaking her shoulder jolted her.

"Oh, Nick! How's Bob? I want to see him."

"He's resting. We'll come back tomorrow. The chief called Sophia. There's nothing for you to do tonight."

Nick carried Nicole in one arm and wrapped the other around Lily's shoulder and they went home.

Chapter Seventeen

Nick laid Nicole on his bed, and Lily went to work changing the saturated diaper. As much as he liked kids, the true extent of his knowledge was limited to riling them up then handing them back to their parents. Having Lily's backup right now was a godsend. Parenthood would be a breeze.

After surrounding Nicole with pillows and taking turns kissing her warm cherub cheeks, they crept into the living room.

Lily turned on the radio and plopped on the couch, while Nick lit a fresh log.

Kneeling before the hearth, he felt her eyes on him, making him conscious of his every move. He glanced over his shoulder and caught her molten stare. She made him feel things he never imagined, as if he was something special. It warmed him from the inside out.

It was more than the romantic ambiance of a slow burning fire, and Keith Richards and the Stones in the background stoking his carnal mood. It was the chemistry of Lily's quiet company and the hum of her body's vibration mingling with his, like a silent dance of the souls. Just being with her was more than enough to keep him happy.

"Well." He sighed after a hectic twenty-four

hours. "Things oughta warm up in a minute." *In more ways than one*. She made room for him on the couch and placed her petite feet in his lap, and he massaged her heels covered in fuzzy socks. He liked everything about her, especially her smallness, which made him feel larger than life.

"That feels *so* good." She sank back against the armrest. "God, next time I get a charley horse you can rub it out for me."

You could rub it out for me, too, only his wicked libido wasn't thinking of a charley horse. Watching her face wince in a glorious mix of pleasure-pain thrilled him to know he could make her feel this way. He could make her feel even better, but he'd wait until they could be alone without a toddler in the other room.

"You really know your way around a baby-bottom, changing diapers and all." He pressed his fingers firmly into her arches.

"It's not exactly rocket science. Just wiping a tiny tush," she answered with a moan and heavy eyelids. "By the way, we should get more milk. And whatever she eats."

"Want me to run out now?"

She shook her head. "Nuh-uh, no way, I don't want you going anywhere. We can make it until tomorrow. Maybe we can take her to the toy store, too. She's gotta be a little homesick by now."

"That's a good idea. You sure you don't mind if she stays here?"

"Not at all. Unless, of course, the new owner kicks me out, then we'll all be looking for a place to sleep. But I don't want you to go. *Ever*." The depth of her words reached her eyes, despite the latest drama. This was no ordinary love or passing fling. This was it.

"About the house…I, uh, don't wanna wear out the welcome." The urge to reveal his secret plan was getting harder to curb.

She silenced him with her index finger against his mouth. "That'll never happen. Trust me." When she straddled his hips and dropped kisses from earlobe to earlobe, under his chin, across his adam's apple, his groin twitched to life. "I want you to stay," she whispered against his skin.

"I'm not going anywhere, sugar." With this raging erection, he'd be lucky if he could stand up. He could've stopped her—would've stopped her—if he wanted to. But he didn't. "You better watch out. You're making me hard right now." Her power worked like kryptonite.

"I know," she breathed, grinding against his jeans. "I can feel it…feel you. Wanna feel me?"

"Yeah." He nodded, just as John Lennon's voice floated into the ether, singing the first line: "*So, this is Christmas…*" He'd never listen to the song the same way again.

She put his hand between her thighs; moist heat radiated through her sweatpants. She wrapped her arms around his neck and kissed him so tenderly he thought he might explode.

So, this is Christmas.

Then she just stopped.

"What?" He examined the drunken smile in her eyes.

"It's just…it feels like forever since I've been so

happy. I forgot how good it could be."

"How good it could be? Or how good it *is*?"

"It *is* good. Isn't it?"

"It'll only get better, I promise, as soon as Nicole is back where she belongs."

Lily stood up, tugging his arm. "Let's go."

"Let's stay." He pulled her back to the couch.

She shook her head. "Nuh-uh. You're coming with me. Dontcha wanna practice making that baby you were talking about?"

****

Lily couldn't stop the baby-making remark from slipping out. She was too turned on; she couldn't turn back if she tried. She didn't want a *gentle* man right now. She wanted Nick's rough and rugged side. Needed to feel him skin-to-skin before she burst.

She lured him to her room and flung him on the bed.

With a familiar smirk curled upon his kissable lips, he fell backward on the mattress, making the old metal frame squeak under his weight. "It's so cold in your room."

"Not for long." She pressed her back to the door until it clicked shut. Then hit the wall switch that turned off the bedside lamp. The streetlight outside her window cast enough of a soft glow to find her target. She yanked off his boots and—despite the urge to fling them—placed them quietly on the floor, not wanting to wake the child across the hall. "A little healthy friction will warm us up, don't you think?"

She sucked in a brave breath as she peeled her sweatshirt over her head, then kicked off her pants.

No way would she waste another night not knowing what it was like to make love to this man.

Her vigorous fingers went straight to work on his belt buckle and zipper, then tossed his jeans aside.

"In a hurry?" The ribbon of light danced in his bemused eyes.

"A little." Every minute without Nick inside her body was like a cold, lonely eternity.

Unwrapping him like a Christmas present, she attacked the shirt buttons and helped him out of the sleeves, then tore off his undershirt. Leaving him in nothing but boxer-briefs and socks, she straddled his hips. His fingers worked the clasp of her bra with an experienced touch.

"Oh, yeah," he murmured with lustful enthusiasm, catching the tip of one aching bud in his mouth.

His suckling sent a shock through her system. When his teeth sank into her tender tip, she squealed from the pleasure-pain. It was raw and animalistic and everything she expected from such a potent man.

"Oh, God." She pulled her breast from his mouth and collapsed on top of him, rubbing her bare skin against his mat of chest hair.

She reached between his legs to stroke the massive erection under his tight briefs, and he pulled her against him, groaning with need. Her cushioned curves coupled with his sinewy strength created a magnetic force—her yin to his yang. With his hands all over her body, she couldn't pry herself away even if she tried.

"Are you sure you're ready?" he rasped.

Parked on his bulge that was thicker than a roll of half-dollar coins, she breathed against his ear, "You're *really* gonna doubt me now?"

"Hell no." He flipped her onto her back, swapping positions with ease. "I hope you don't mind but I like being on top."

She ought to be scared to death for starting this. But she felt fantastic, like floating on a champagne cloud. She stretched out languidly on the flimsy old mattress.

"Let's get rid of these." He plucked her slouching socks. "And these." He peeled down her panties, an inch at a time, teasing her, when all she wanted was for him to tear them off. His knuckles grazed her inner thighs, going up one then down the other.

Her over-sensitized nerves sizzled like hot bubbles popping under her skin. She clamped her lips shut to stifle her shriek and pressed her hips to the blanket. When he spread her legs wide, bending a knee over each of his shoulders, she crushed her eyelids together, peeking through her lashes, awaiting his next move.

"Hmm, flexible." With his face between her thighs, he smacked his lips like some kind of starving beast. "Mind if I go down on you first?"

Lily held her breath. "Uhh, okay, why not?"

He chuckled. "That doesn't sound like a yes."

"It's just...I'm not used to someone's face in my...crotch."

"Well, you better get used to it." He took her foot and massaged the insole.

Her whole body arched at the exquisite touch,

more sensual than his previous foot rub. When he dropped kisses along her instep, over her ankle, and up her calf, she squeaked. She'd never been kissed behind the knee before and she loved it.

Once he covered the right leg, he started the same treatment on the left, beginning with her toes. She fought the urge to giggle by clenching the sheet. By the time he finished lavishing both legs her head was swirling.

Then his lips worked their way toward the aching valley between her thighs, stealing a taste with his tongue.

"Wait!" She nearly catapulted off the bed trying to escape, but his arms kept her locked in place.

He poked up his head for a moment to say, "Too late," before diving down again and putting his warm mouth against her. His fingers parted the fleshy folds as he lapped slow, easy, and deep, tickling her sweet spot with his extraordinary kiss.

All she could do was hang on and enjoy the magnificent ride, moaning in ecstasy. Her misty mind was a double rainbow of light, a crowded void filled with everything and nothing at all. Just Nick. His mouth. Her body.

Mark never did this. Until now, she had no idea why anyone would ever do this. It was nothing like she imagined it to be, making her shatter into an endless sea of stars behind her eyelids.

"No more. I can't take it. Please, stop." Instinct had her stiffening her leg muscles around his head.

"Just relax. Let me finish."

"Oh, but it feels so-so… Ooh-ooh-ooh…"

She restrained her scream while he worked her

body into a willowy, pliable tizzy with his lips, teeth and tongue. It was a sensual tug-of-war. She pushed her pelvis into his face while tugging his head away from her crotch—ending in a climactic collision unlike anything she'd ever known. She struggled to open her eyes blurred by bliss.

He inched up to meet her gaze, his smile glistening with her wet heat. Panting, from the hard labor of making love with his mouth, or his overall pent-up sexual frustration—or both—he asked, "Are you ready for the real deal?"

Her attention fell from his face to the unfathomably enormous phallus with a droplet of moisture glistening from the pink tip. From her vantage point, it was massive, like a roll of cookie dough, or just looked that way from this angle. It made her vibrator look like a bread stick. She was no virgin, but still, it was hard to believe the size of the fully erect, naked thing. Harder to imagine how it would fit inside her.

"Don't worry, sugar. I'll make it feel good. I promise," he whispered.

What did she do to deserve this ready, willing, and able man? He could do anything he wanted with her body. Anything at all. "I know you will."

He nodded to the box of condoms on the nightstand. "How do you want it? With or without. Your call."

The question made her stomach flip.

Even with her cloudy consciousness, Lily was acutely aware of her monthly cycle; she was due any day, getting pregnant was improbable.

But, in the odd chance she did, what could go

wrong? Nothing could be more wonderful than having Nick's baby.

"Without."

****

If Nick were a gambling man, he would have bet it all on Lily requesting the condom.

After all, she bought 'em.

Went through hell with Sophia because of 'em.

And now they weren't gonna use 'em.

After all the baby talk, she finally was on the same page, in the same book.

But he couldn't help but wonder if she knew what she was doing in the heat of the moment. Just like men, women were capable of some crazy things when the blood left the brain.

Poised between her parted thighs, he was almost afraid to take her with the frightened, glassy look in her eyes, somewhere between shock, and awe, and flat-out disbelief, as if she was lost in another dimension.

Still, it didn't prevent him from taking his erection in-hand, aiming for the target. He wanted nothing more than to slide it in, but she was so tight, it would tear her in half.

Her whole body clenched, bracing for the painful penetration. What a good sport she was, letting him have his way with her body; he wanted it to be good for her too and take her all the way to heaven.

He bent over to snatch a kiss from her lips before pulling back to examine her flushed skin and far-out dazed eyes. "Feeling good?"

"Yeah. I am." Her languid voice was deeper,

raspier, and sexier than any time before. He liked her like this. Wet. Willing. And waiting.

"Let me know if I hurt you. Okay?" He leaned back on his haunches to study her face for any signs of doubt.

"Oo-kay," she repeated like she was lost in a dream.

His hand cupped between her legs, rechecking her heat. "God…you're an inferno."

Then his middle finger slid across the slick spot where his tongue had enjoyed the flavor of her tangy sweetness, where his aching flesh longed to be. Like a key in her ignition, his finger turned her on and she hummed with new life, so he dipped it in deep.

Her soft, snug walls surrounded it, milking it; his rigid arousal twitched in anticipation of being next in line.

"What are you waiting for?" she teased, flicking her tongue across her swollen bottom lip.

He pushed the finger inside again until his palm was flat against her and she fell back on the pillow exhaling a carnal cry. Then he pulled it out fast, giving her a moment to recover while her motel eyes begged for more.

"Don't stop," she whimpered.

Eager to please, he drove his finger inside again, as far as it could go. She nearly bunny-hopped off the bed, but he held her in place not letting her get away. In and out, her hips found the rhythm of his hand, while her breath came in sharp, shallow waves.

She handled one finger like a champion.

Clamping her hands around his wrist in a desperate attempt to control the pace, she seemed to know how she wanted it, because in a hot flash he felt the wet eruption of orgasm number two.

She might be done, but he was just getting started. To prevent her motor from shutting down he slipped in two fingers, making her groan and gyrate harder. By the third finger, she was howling into a pillow. He hoped she was ready for him.

"You okay?" he asked, uncovering her face.

She nodded, hardly breathing at all, gritting her teeth, while her eyelashes fluttered wildly.

"Don't hold back. Just let it out. I wanna hear you. Don't worry about Nicole. She can't hear a thing," he lied. "You want more?"

Panting, she nodded, squirming against the sheets. "Yes."

"I don't wanna hurt you. You can barely handle three fingers…"

"Just. Do. It."

Knowing Mother Nature has a way of making things work out, he thrust into her.

She moaned softly against his chest, shattering his soul. Convulsing beneath him, she gripped his shoulders, wincing and whimpering.

"Tell me if you want me to stop."

"Don't. Stop."

Still, he pushed in deeper, and she accepted the full-length of him, her sugar walls milking his sensitized stiffness. God, he could explode right now simply being inside her. But he held back, wanting it to last, wanting her to finish first, if she could manage to come again.

Pulling out slowly, taking his time to withdraw the shaft, leaving only the tip inside, he asked, "Does it hurt?" He arched back so he could see the truth in her eyes with the fraction of light spilling through the window.

She nodded. "A little. But it's not your fault, I mean, you're huge. And it's also been such a long time since I've been with a man."

"It'll hurt less if I do it fast."

"Okay." She anchored her arms around his biceps. "I'm ready."

He drove in again, quicker this time, in and out, a little faster each time.

She gasped, biting his chest to stifle her scream.

If he kissed her, to help take her mind off the pressure, he'd wind up hurting her by stretching her into a more painful position. All he could do at this point was keep at it until it felt as good for her as it did for him.

With her legs wrapped around his waist and her hands pulling down his torso, she urged him even deeper inside her, rocking together, pounding in perfect rhythm. Another few minutes of riding her like this would kill him.

"I can't hold it," he breathed.

Aching pleasure twisted her face as she bucked against him, moaning, "Oh, yes! Yes. Yes. Yesss..." singing in time to his orgasm.

"Oh, yeah, sugar. That's what I'm talking about. Let it out." He groaned against her hair, tugging a fistful, until the vigorous vibration ended the glorious ride.

Chapter Eighteen

Weak from the aftershock of Nick's intense lovemaking, Lily couldn't move anything but her eyeballs. Lying awake in the crook of his sinewy, strong arm, the darkness developed into a pale gray through the white eyelet curtain shimmying in the draft.

He was so *skilled.* There wasn't an inch of her left untouched, unadorned with his kisses, unmoved by his mastery. Her love-sore, listless body was paying the price for his expertise.

Her overactive, yet surprisingly calm mind, drifted in and out of consciousness, until orange slices of sun burned like laser beams across her face making sleep impossible.

She kicked off the blanket, but Nick readjusted their arrangement into a tight spooning position, snaking his sturdy leg over hers, weaving his foot between her ankles.

Okay, fine. She didn't want to get out of bed anyway.

A sated smile tugged her tired lips. God, even her face hurt from the friction burn of his rough stubble. Her inner thighs suffered the same soreness.

She'd forgotten how the human touch could be so...so much more invigorating than a battery-operated vibrator.

With his love-gun nestled against her derrière like it was his holster, she considered going for round three but wasn't sure she could handle another dose of his super sexual stamina.

Although, if he made the right moves, no doubt she'd let him ride her every which way 'til Wednesday.

His fantastic fire hose twitched against the small of her back, and she braced herself for another flaming-hot, soul-baring, mind-blowing ride on Cloud 9.

However, across the hall, there was a mouse stirring.

Lily gave Nick a gentle elbow to the ribs. "Nicole's awake."

The only response was a light snore and his thick arm crushing her like a boa constrictor.

"Nick? Did you hear me? We oughta get dressed before she sees us like this."

He made a sleepy smack of his lips and rolled over, releasing his grip.

She sprang out of bed, wincing when her bare feet hit the chilled floor, realizing the extent of the pain. Everything ached, from her scalp to her calves. The simple action of reaching for her bathrobe on the hook beside her bedroom door and bending over to slip on a fresh pair of socks was agonizing.

Needing a tall order of aspirin, Ben-Gay, and plenty of java for breakfast, she shuffled to the kitchen, avoiding the partially open door to Nick's room, unprepared to deal with Nicole without some caffeine in her system first. She also wanted to call the hospital to check on Bob without having to explain the baby in the background.

No wonder the house was freezing. The fire was out, the thermostat was set to sixty-two degrees, and the arctic air piercing through the kitchen window was enough to rattle the curtains. On tiptoes, she struggled to close the gap, but without enough leverage, it wouldn't budge.

"Forget it," she grumbled, giving up.

She turned on the oven and opened the door for an instant blast of heat. While the coffee brewed, she started a load of laundry.

At the sound of little feet stomping down the hallway, Lily drained the last drop of milk into the Sippy cup. Then she gulped black coffee, and shuddered before digging a powdered creamer from a gift basket.

Looking like a little angry refugee with matted hair, Nicole climbed onto a chair at the kitchen table. "Nuk!"

"Well, good morning to you too, sunshine." Lily handed the girl the cup, not letting the toddler-sized attitude get on her nerves so early in the day. "Guess what we're doing later."

Sucking viciously on the mouthpiece, Nicole stared blankly.

"We're going shopping."

"Go chopping now!" Nicole slammed the cup on the table.

"Excuse me?"

"Go now!" Nicole snapped back with milk trailing down her chin.

Lily dropped a bowl of dry cereal on the table

just as Nick appeared. "Thank God, you're up."

"No want 'dis." The demon-child flipped the bowl into the air.

"Good morning, ladies. What the *hell's* going on in here?" he said, calmly.

"Oh, nothing. Just having some yummy breakfast on the floor." Lily's patience was wearing thin.

"Chopping! Chopping!" Nicole chanted. "Go chopping now!"

Nick nodded. "Yeah, yeah, so I heard. But this is how it's gonna work—coffee first, shopping later…Actually, fire first."

He lit another log while Lily filled his cup. Then she grabbed a broom and swept the Cheerios into a pile.

"And shut this *damn* window." He brushed aside the curtain panels blowing in the breeze and pressed down on the wooden frame. "I'm gonna nail this thing closed," he mumbled. Then he snapped off the oven, cut his eyes at Lily, and gave her a disapproving headshake. "I told you to quit heating the house like this. It's dangerous."

She responded with her best apologetic eyes, knowing he was right, handing him a coffee mug like a peace offering.

He took it in exchange for a quick peck on the lips. "Feeling okay today?"

Heat creep up her cheeks. "Yeah, of course. I, um, I feel great."

"Me, too." He gave her a wicked smile. "I'll take over in here while you get dressed."

After a quick shower, she studied her figure in

the full-length bedroom mirror, imagining her flat tummy the size of a basketball, then quickly waved the ridiculous idea away. She might be ready for Nick but she wasn't ready for a baby.

He knocked twice on her bedroom door without coming in. "You ready?" In the background, Nicole was whining about something.

"Five minutes," she sang.

"Meet us in the truck."

Lily smoothed her hair, arranging it around her neck to hide the hickey on the soft spot above her collarbone.

The unopened condom box on the nightstand caught her attention, had her thinking…

Worrying…

She studied at the calendar on the wall. Her period was due any moment, if her calculations were correct.

But what if I'm wrong?

Deciding to have a baby isn't something to commit to over a bowl of ice cream. It requires planning. At the very least, it should involve an engagement ring, or better yet a wedding ring.

Recalling the night at Brawny's Farm, the mother with the swollen belly and her three unmanageable kids.

Babysitting was one thing.

Having a baby was…completely different.

Completely scary.

The hyperventilating started, so she grabbed the Farley's Pharmacy paper bag and breathed into it.

After two months of knowing Nick—half of which she spent trying to forget him—how the hell did she let that man talk her into having a baby?

With her heart and hopes sinking, she called the doctor on speed-dial. "Anytime today, just walk in," the receptionist said.

Meanwhile, Lily vowed to keep quiet unless Nick brought it up first. And even then, she wasn't sure what to say. She could hardly think straight, let alone prepare herself for the inevitable conversation.

She climbed into the truck, brushing aside windblown bangs from her eyes, and Nick did a double take. "Wow. Don't you look pretty? You're glowing." He stared at her for long moment before putting the truck in Reverse.

Glowing? What the hell does that mean? Maybe her face was still red from his beard stubble.

The ride to the mall took twice as long with the traffic. Thank God, the radio was loud enough to occupy everybody's attention with cheerful Christmas carols. The parking lot was maxxed out by noon, so they took a spot a mile away.

"You're awfully quiet. You sure you're okay?"

"I'm just tired." She slid out of the truck and hunkered down against the icy air.

He snatched a runaway shopping cart and stuffed Nicole in the front seat. "Let's go shopping, baby!"

They stepped out of the frigid air, through the automatic doors, into the stifling heat of Child World. It was hard to maintain the Christmas spirit while being shoved by frantic shoppers in the Africa-hot inferno.

Nick tore down the aisle, zigzagging like a racecar out of control with Nicole squealing in delight.

With a loaded mind, Lily trailed behind, unable to envision anything else but the potential father in this good man. *Would it really be so bad if I were pregnant?*

When the baby dolls came into view, Nicole freaked out.

"We're just getting one toy today. You gotta ask Santa Claus for the rest." Nick winked at Lily.

When Nicole spied the indoor play area, she chucked the doll and screamed, "Wanna go 'dare!"

Nick plucked her out of the cart and she ran to the ball pit.

"Do you think that's such a good idea?" Lily asked.

He rolled his eyes. "Why? Do you have something against having fun?"

"No, of course not. But I do have something against germs."

"Oh, God," Nick snorted. "Don't tell me you're gonna be one of those overprotective mothers?"

Dodging the mom-remark, not wanting to jinx the chance her period might still be on the way, Lily returned fire with a glower of her own. "I bet that pit is brewing like a Petri dish. I'd be shocked if we don't leave here with the chicken pox."

"Aw, come on. It's only a ball pit." Nick sat on an empty bench overlooking the play area and pulled Lily with him. "Besides, I already had the chicken pox."

"Me, too. But what about her? Do you even know if she's up-to-date on her vaccinations?"

"I appreciate your concern." He dropped a kiss on her forehead. "Just leave the worrying to me, okay?" His smile was so sincere, Lily felt guilty for her negative thoughts. "I just want a minute alone to talk to you." He pressed her hands between both of his.

"Can't it wait 'til later when Nicole's sleeping?" She wasn't ready for words; she wanted to discuss things with her doctor first.

"I just need to tell you how happy I am right now. *You* make me happy."

Lily went limp with his tender tone.

In the middle of Child World, out of the blue, he said, "I love you, Lily. I really, really do."

Lost in the deep, dark pools of his eyes, feeling his words, she believed them with her whole heart. If it weren't for the lump clogging her throat, she would have said she loved him, too.

"You don't have to say it back. I just wanted you to know what I'm feeling." He hugged her for a few blissful moments. "Well, I've had enough of this place. I'm ready to go home. Come on, Nicole."

Observing more than a dozen kids bouncing around made it difficult to pinpoint the one they were looking for.

"Do you see her?" Nick shot up to get an overview of the miniature mob.

Lily's heart felt like a cold stone in her chest. "She was right there—" She pointed a shaky finger to place she'd last seen the child before Nick derailed her with his sweet-talk. "Nicole?"

Nick searched the vicinity while Lily ran to get a security guard.

When she returned, he was hugging the toddler with fright still straining his face. "She was right behind the bench. A foot away. In the clothes rack."

"Happens all the time," the guard said.

"Thank God," was all Lily could say. "Thank God. Thank God." Over and over all the way back to Scenic View.

"Are you okay?" he asked, his face a pale mask of stupefied concern.

"My nerves are shot."

"Mine, too."

"I never lost a kid in a store before. Kinda freaked me out."

"Kinda? I think I have an ulcer after that scare."

"Mind if we stop in town? I want to run to the pharmacy," she said without further explanation of her covert mission.

He parked along the curb and gave her a hundred dollar bill. "Get some antacid for me. Nicole and I will pick up some milk at the mini-mart."

She snuck into Farley's to buy a pregnancy test. *Am I nuts? If the word about the condoms spread so fast, a pregnancy test would be like wildfire.* She paid for the antacid then slipped out the back door, ran behind the building, down the alley, across the street, and a block to the doctor's office.

Doctor Kramer listened as Lily rambled. "I just lost a toddler in the store. I don't think I'm ready for this yet," her voice wavered. She hugged her backpack in her lap like a security blanket. "Can you give me a pregnancy test now?"

"You'll need to wait a few days to get an accurate reading. You might be worrying for nothing, which could delay your cycle. What exactly are you here for? My professional advice or to take action?"

Lily shrugged.

The doctor rummaged through a cabinet and brought some items to his desk.

"This is the morning-after pill. You can take it now, up to seventy-two hours after intercourse and stop the worry—*if* that's why you're here. Or..." He pushed the prenatal vitamins and smiled. "You can take these and be worrying the rest of your life. And in case you're not pregnant after all." He gave her a starter pack of birth control pills and a sample of condoms.

The options were overwhelming.

The morning-after pill was *definitely* out of the question. And if she were pregnant, it was too late for birth control. She shook the bottle of vitamins that sounded like a big baby rattle.

"Are you considering spending your life with this man?"

She nodded, afraid to admit it aloud, not wanting to jinx herself.

"I'm only asking because I think I've known you long enough to be frank. Make the right decision for yourself. If he's not interested in being a father, and you can't do it as a single parent, there are couples out there ready to welcome a new baby into their lives."

She wanted to say Nick *was* interested, but the words were lost in her hazy head.

"So, you've got more options than just these pills." He gathered everything into a small brown bag, which Lily stuffed into her backpack. "Plus," he said, sounding hopeful as he showed her to the door, "there's always the chance that this is a false alarm."

****

Staring into the raging fire, unable to sleep, Nick's mind replayed those few agonizing moments of losing Nicole. He tried not to imagine all the horrible *what-ifs* that could have gone wrong and fortunately didn't.

His stomach tightened.

Even though the security guard confirmed it happened all the time, Nick still felt like an irresponsible jerk. He'd done the same sort of shenanigans as a kid. No wonder his mother split. Who needs the aggravation?

How could he imagine being a father when he almost lost his godchild?

He still hadn't told Tristan, who trusted his daughter was safer with Nick than with anyone. Wait until he finds out. It wasn't the sort of conversation to have over the phone. *Maybe Tristan won't be too pissed. Who'm I kiddin'? I'd kill him if he lost my baby.*

Just thinking about it drove Nick to survey the child asleep in his bed.

Then he checked on Lily, in the fetal position facing the wall. He wanted to thank her again for so many things, most of all for her recent support with Nicole. No doubt, she'd make a great mother someday. For now, he'd dial down on the baby talk before he overloaded her emotional circuits.

"Lily?" He gave her leg a little motivating shake, hoping she'd waken. When she didn't respond, he backed out of her room quietly.

He grabbed can of soda from the fridge, cracked the tab, and sipped the effervescent overflow. No matter how hard he tried, there was fooling his brain into believing it was a beer. He swiped the foam from his disillusioned mouth with a tight fist, debating if he should take his frustration out on the drafty window shaking the curtains like a ghost.

Nailing the damn thing shut would cut the piercing stream of air squeezing under the warped wood. But sealing it would create another hazard this firetrap couldn't afford.

This place needed it all. Windows. Heating system. Electrical system. *Everything.*

He already made a list and sketched out a few ideas. But nothing would happen until after the holiday.

Contemplating Christmas had his mood in an upswing.

They never got around to decorating the tree today. So he strung up the lights while the girls slept. In the morning, they could add the ornaments.

After draping the branches with strands of multi-colored twinkling bulbs, he stood back to admire his handiwork, tripping on Lily's backpack tucked in the dark corner.

A few things spilled out of the open zipper, including a brown paper bag that rattled like a can full of beans. He rummaged inside, his serious sweet tooth expecting jellybeans despite being the wrong season for Easter candy.

All he found were...pills? *Prenatal what*? He beamed in delight.

Next, he pulled out a disk of birth control pills, followed by a sample-sized package of condoms. A disappointed lump filled this throat.

He shook the bag to ensure it was empty. But there was something else. Something small.

A tiny foil bubble-package containing a single white pill spilled into his hand. He tried reading the small words in the glow of the Christmas lights before going to the kitchen where it was brighter.

"What the hell is *this*!" His heart deflated.

Lily intended to stop a pregnancy that probably hadn't even started. Why? What about everything they talked about?

His potential future just turned inside out. Gritting his teeth, he stomped toward Lily's bedroom with his temper roiling beyond his control and the foil pouch crushed in his fist.

He rumbled through her bedroom like a freight train. "Lily! I wanna talk to you." He slammed the door. When she didn't move, he simply flipped her onto her back and put his nose to hers, shaking her shoulders, making it impossible for her to sleep through this wake up call. "Get. Up!"

"I don't feel like talking. I have a headache."

"Here. Take a pill." He opened his fist, revealing what was inside.

"What's that?" It was too dark to see so he turned on the bedside lamp.

Stewing in his own acidic juices, he blurted out, "When were you gonna tell me about this?"

She rolled over and mumbled into the pillow, "Never."

"What do you mean, *never*?" He flipped her over again and sat her upright. "When did you get *this*?"

"Today. I ran over to the doctor's office when you dropped me at the pharmacy. If I wanted you to know I would have told you."

He never expected her to be so sneaky. "Why don't you want me to know?"

She shrugged. "Because, my period is due any minute. I doubt I'm even pregnant."

"Then what's this for?" He held up the poisonous pill. "Insurance purposes?"

"Nick..." Lily went limp, sobbing into her hands.

She looked so pitiful, he almost felt sorry for her. He never would have made love without protection if she hadn't agreed to it. "You're just overwhelmed. Once Nicole goes home and it's just the two of us..."

"You keep saying 'when we're alone.' How long do you think it'll last—us being alone—if I'm pregnant?"

"It'll be different when it's our baby."

She squinted like she was trying to see the future in his face. "Are you really ready for a baby? Or are you just afraid if you don't have one now you never will?" she asked, weakly. "Shouldn't we know each other little longer before bringing a child into the world?"

His heart sank. "So, what—you *don't* want to have a baby with me?"

Lily shook her head. "I didn't say that. Maybe now's not the right time."

"Well, then, you better take the damn pill so we can forget everything that happened." He bit a hole in the foil and held the white dot to her lips.

"No!" She smacked his hand away.

"Yes!" He stuck it in her mouth and she bit his

finger in the process. "What the—"

"Pfth." She spat, and it bounced off his chest and rolled under the dresser.

Torn between strangling her and making love to her, he fumed. "Whatja do that for?"

She cut her eyes as she pushed herself off the bed and inched toward the door. "I'm not making any decisions right now."

Outraged by her nonchalance, he grabbed her elbow, spinning her into his arms. He caught the familiar glow of lust in her eyes. Heavy breathing flared her nostrils. She wasn't nearly as infuriated as she seemed. He felt the vibration of her pulse as rampant as his own. Her pheromonal heat wave started a chemical combustion that aroused his beast. Blood gushed from his pounding heart straight to his throbbing groin as he crushed her against the bedroom door with his mouth to hers.

Thank God, she kissed back with equal hunger as he stripped her, not giving her a second to resist. Then he shoved his pants down. When he picked her up, she wrapped her arms and legs around him.

"Good girl," he growled.

She purred as he tested her readiness with one…two…three fingers…

Once she was revved up, he drove it home, riding her wild and free, rougher than he intended, impressed at how well she handled it.

"Oh. No. Yeah. Please," she whimpered.

He paused at her string of airy contradictions. "What's it gonna be, sugar? Yes. Or no?"

Nose-to-nose, she shrugged, and a sly, spiteful smile glimmered in her eyes.

"Okay. You wanna play games. I can play games, too." He flexed his solid strength until her walls milked him for more.

She squealed, holding him tight.

"Tell me how you want it."

"Hard..." she groaned.

Manipulating her body was easy. She clung to him, as he rearranged their vertical position without pulling out, dropping to the cold, hard floor. On his hands and knees, he rocked into her.

"I'd marry you in a heartbeat—you know that? I. Would. I. Will." He thrust with each word. Deeper. Longer. Stronger.

She tore off his t-shirt and dug her nails into his shoulders. Bucking against him with her own great strength, she forced him to work at her rhythm until a ripple ran through her body. He felt her contractions come first before releasing into her.

When they pulled apart, he noticed the ruddy stain glistened on the shaft. "Look..."

"That's from sex, not from my cycle."

"I'm sorry." His heart stopped when he thought he'd hurt her.

"I'm...fine."

He wiped his spent flesh with his t-shirt before pulling on his jeans, then handed her the bathrobe as she recuperated on the floor.

She reached under the dresser, came out with a hand full of dust bunnies, and tried blowing the fuzz off the pill.

Bing! His blood pressure skyrocketed again. "Wait! So, you're still gonna take it?"

"I'm not doing anything tonight." With a tight

fist, Lily crawled back into bed.

"Well, I'm not sticking around to find out what you *choose* to do. I'm outta here." He cleared his stuff from the spare room, grabbed Nicole, and hit the road.

Chapter Nineteen

Packing cardboard boxes was supposed to keep Lily too busy to think of Nick, but it only made her think more...about everything. Sorting this junk was a struggle—what she needed was a dumpster! She didn't have the heart to put the Christmas tree with the trash, so to avoid looking at it she'd dragged it to the backyard.

Ten days passed since their fight, and the pain was still fresh from the open wound she'd brought upon herself. She missed him like crazy. He probably still hated her now as much as that night.

Could she blame him? She gave him every reason to leave with her ambiguous attitude. But she hadn't been in the mood for baby talk and was too scared to deal with her mixed emotions. The plan was to let nature take its course...but then Nick found the pill, and everything went to hell.

Her period came the next day, right on schedule. She'd saved the tablet as proof, just in case he returned. But he didn't.

The piercing scream of a fire truck caused a tremor down her spine. "Dear God, please keep him safe," she prayed. Then she planted her face in her hands to catch another flow of uncontrollable tears. She was exhausted from sobbing for days and nights.

It came in pitiful waves and right now was high tide. Her cheeks and runny nose were painfully raw from swiping them with another rough tissue.

A rap on the screen door jolted her from the pity party. She sucked in a breath, anticipating for a single second that it might be him. She pressed her face to the living room window, surprised, and a little disappointed, to see Bob on her front step. Since the heart attack, his doctor told him to take it easy, so he closed the shop indefinitely.

"Everything okay?" Lily let him inside with a feigned smile.

"Yeah, yeah," Bob mumbled, followed by a tall, tanned man with chunky blonde streaks in his long blown-back hair. "Everything's fine. I feel great—better than ever. This is Bruno." He rolled his eyes at his companion. "Sophia's *nephew* from California. We just came from the parade."

"Oh, it was today? I forgot." That was a big lie.

"I tried calling you but the operator said your phone's disconnected."

"I was getting too many wrong numbers," she lied again.

"Are you going to the Christmas party?"

"Oh, no, I, um, I can't."

"Sure you can. It starts at five. You have an hour to get dressed."

"I'm…packing."

"Already?"

"Yep. The house is sold. The real estate agent called Wednesday with the news. Isn't that great?" The forced words hurt her heart as she said them aloud for the first time. "It happened so fast, they must've really wanted it because they offered twice my price."

"Who bought it?"

She shrugged. "I don't know. And I don't care. I let the attorney handle all that stuff. It was an anonymous investor as far as I know. They paid cash and gave me an open-ended move date."

"I guess they're not in any hurry to get in then," Bruno said, glancing around with a disgusted look screwing up his otherwise decent face. "I can see why. It needs a lot of work. They're probably waiting for spring so they can knock it down."

"*Ya think?*" Lily wanted to smack the smugness right out of him. Sophia's nephew had the disposition of a loaded diaper.

"What happened to your *roommate?*" Bob asked.

"He found another place." She omitted all the details and fought the urge to cry.

"If you need help moving boxes, I'm sure Bruno wouldn't mind."

"Whoa, Unc—" Bruno put up his palms. "I'm here on *vay-cay*. I'm not a moving man."

"Shut up, *stunata*. Your aunt would smack you in the mouth if she heard you talking so stupid. Sorry Lily, he has the looks but lacks the manners."

"Can I use your bathroom?" Bruno asked.

She pointed down the hall.

"He probably wants to check his makeup. Sophia made him my nursemaid until she gets back from Florida. Do me a favor and come to the party so I don't have to get stuck with that lug the whole time."

Lily hemmed and hawed. "Oh, fine." It was time to deliver her Christmas presents to the lucky recipients anyway. And deep down she wanted a reason to go just to see Nick again.

****

After bouncing the last kid on his knee, Santa Claus stretched his sore thighs. Nick's legs hadn't hurt this much since he had Lily on the bedroom floor. He missed her so much he could barely breathe.

Ever since storming out that night everything seemed to ache. His head. His heart. And his ego.

It was her body, and her right to do what she wanted. He was wrong to come on so viciously and regretted it as soon as he bolted out her door. But he couldn't go back—not while she was so…detached; and he was so heartbroken by an unattainable dream.

Even though Nicole went home the next day, he decided to stay at the Scenic View Inn until his super-deluxe customer camper arrived. He didn't want to tell Maresca how he screwed things up. And he wasn't sure how to fix it.

Maybe Lily would be in a forgiving mood now that her financial crisis was resolved. If he got the nerve, he'd go by her house tonight to see if she'd accept his apology for everything and be willing to try again from scratch.

Waiting for Santa's cue to leave, he spotted the familiar redhead and his broken heart swelled with new hope. Then he noticed the stranger hovering beside her and made a beeline in their direction.

Over the din and holiday music Lily's new friend jibed, "Ho-ho-ho! Look who's in town? Where's your reindeer, Fat Man?"

"Ho-ho-ho, yourself, pal."

"Hey, Kris Kringle, what's your problem?"

I'm looking at it. Seething, Nick wished he were in his street clothes rather than this ridiculous getup.

"Aww, come on, *chillax*. What's the matter—got a lump of coal up your ass or something?" The guy put a playful paw on Santa's shoulder.

"Get your hand off me, *Fabio*."

"Nick!" Lily blinked stormy eyes. "You don't have to be so rude! This is Bruno, Sophia's nephew."

"Oh, is that right?" Nick flipped the pom-pom from the Santa cap out of his eye to get a better look at the competition. "So, you're the infamous *golden ticket*, huh?" His fists tensed at his side.

"What's that supposed to mean?" Oblivious to the tense situation, Bruno asked Lily, "You know this guy?"

"She's my girlfriend."

Lily glared at him. "Was! *Was* your girlfriend."

"Whoa, you're, like, sleeping with Santa?" Bruno hooted. "That's hilarious. Are you blowing the Easter Bunny, too?"

"Don't talk to her like that!" Nick rumbled on the verge of eruption.

"Oh, get over yourself, old man. I'm just funning around with her. Maybe we can get a three-way with the Tooth Fairy, whaddaya say?" Bruno winked and put his arm around Lily.

"I told you to watch your mouth!" Reeling back, Nick socked Bruno square in the jaw, knocking the veneers off his front teeth.

"Nick! What the hell are ya doin'?" Maresca shouted. "Quick, get the kids outta here. Now!"

Bob chuckled. "Nice shot, Santa. I bet now all

he'll want for Christmas is his two front teeth."

"Are you nuts? What kind of Santa are you?" Bruno got up and swiped his hand across his bloody mouth. "I'm outtie."

Repulsion twisted Lily's face. "What's wrong with you? You didn't have to hit him!"

"Lily, I'm sorry." He wanted to grab her, hug her, smother her with kisses, but she just backed away, shaking her head. "Look, I didn't mean to beat up your date."

"He's not my date!" She scowled, mumbling some insults under her breath before darting out the door.

****

Despite the darkness and harsh wind, Lily dared the slippery climb home. Her jaw ached from non-stop chattering, and her cheeks were numb from warm tears gone bitter cold. Frozen air penetrated her velour track pants like millions of icy-hot pinpricks, making her thighs itch and burn.

She'd be lucky if she didn't get frostbite.

For now, she just considered herself stupid for making the journey on foot when she could have found a ride home since Bruno didn't offer one.

Her broken heart wished the headlights aiming at her might be Nick coming to make amends, but when the big truck sped by, dousing her with dirty bits of slush, she realized it wasn't him.

"Just. Keep. Walking." She huffed and puffed white clouds.

Aside from a roaring fire, which she no longer had, immersing her body in a steaming bath would be the quickest way to defrost these bones. She hoped the water heater would cooperate this one time, otherwise she'd have to settle for a quick shower.

At the top of the hill, the bungalow sparkled under the streetlights like a crystal-covered beacon in the night.

So sad it belonged to someone else now.

As soon as she stumbled over the threshold, she ran to the bathroom, dropped the stopper in the drain, and turned the spigot. Rising steam warmed her cheeks, and she ran her hands underneath the flow until the feeling returned to her fingers.

While the tub filled, she peeled out of the wet clothes in front of the hot oven. She grabbed the leftover bottle of room-temperature champagne, popped the cork, and chugged it. Not a celebratory drink on any level. This was purely medicinal.

The morning-after pill sat in a shot glass by the kitchen sink, next to the little green candle—more painful reminders of what could have been.

Maybe if Nick knew she didn't take it he'd forgive her for doubting him. For doubting herself.

Showing her face at the Christmas party proved to be a stupid idea. But his jealousy gave her some satisfaction. He even called her his present-tense girlfriend, as if that meant anything to either of them now...

Maybe it did. Maybe it wasn't too late to fix this after all.

If she hadn't disconnected her telephone in a hasty attempt to move out and fall off the radar, she could have called him. Now she wished she'd hadn't made herself purposely unreachable. A dumb move considering she hadn't paid her cell phone bill in months and the service was finally cut off.

Wishing was pointless.

Or was it?

Candles were for making wishes—that's what Nick said. So maybe the votive from VV's had the power to make a wish come true and bring him back.

She struck a match, but the airy draft blew out it out. "Humph," she snorted, wondering if it was some kind of sign. She tried again and it worked.

Staring at the tiny flame dancing in the saucer on the counter, she watched the melting wax pool around the wick. It smelled just like Christmas. And reminded her of Nick and that night in the dressing room...

Splashing from the bathroom brought her back to the moment, so she ran to check the tub. It was only half-full, but at least the water was hot. She closed the door to conserve the steam before stepping in and slipping under the surface, letting the water work its magic. An instant mind-erasing, stress relieving, bone-defrosting soak was just what she needed.

She dozed until the water turned cool.

Until—

A distinct burning odor seeped in. Then thin wisps of smoke curled under the bathroom door.

"Oh, my God!"

She shot to her feet with water sluicing down her body. The door was hot to the touch. Smoke continued leaking in, so she dunked the towel in the tub and stuffed it along the bottom.

There was plywood covering up the little broken

window over the toilet, and she pounded it until her hands were raw. But it was no use. She was trapped.

She wrapped herself in Nick's flannel shirt, which still hung on the hook behind bathroom door just where he'd left it, like a symbol of hope that he might return for it one day.

Then she crouched in the corner—crying, praying—and waited to die.

****

Once Maresca kicked Santa out of the building for ruining the party, Nick didn't even bother to change his clothes. He didn't want to waste another moment. He only wanted to see Lily.

First, he needed to get his mind around what he would say when she opened the door. *If* she opened the door. He took the scenic route, giving him more time to update his apology.

Maybe if he told her about the size of his bank account she'd forgive him for everything. He'd even rethink his commitment to the fire department if it meant that much to her. Ideas churned while his tires crawled up the slick slope of Sunflower Summit.

The closer he got to her house, the stronger the familiar acrid odor in the air became. A plume of white filled the inky sky, blocking out the stars. Out of curiosity, he picked up the radio and asked the dispatcher, "Anyone report a fire?"

Without waiting for feedback, he unbuttoned the red jacket as he drove. Pulled off the white beard. Ripped apart the Velcro tabs holding the fake padded belly around his waist. Something in his gut told him it was Lily's house, and he was right.

"Dammit!"

Sirens in the distance were a mile away when he jumped out of the truck and grabbed his safety gear. He kicked off the Santa boots, then stepped into his firefighting boots. Hiked the trousers over the red pants and shrugged on the suspenders. Whipped the turnout coat over his undershirt. Strapped on his respiratory mask and helmet. Pulled on his gloves. Threw the fireproof blanket over his shoulder. And, with the extinguisher and the Halligan tool in his hands, he ran toward the inferno.

His adrenaline bubble burst once he pried open the front door and a noxious black cloud escaped. He smashed the living room window to release more smoke, but there was still too much to see anything beyond his nose. The extinguisher was ineffective in a case like this; only a hose could control this blaze.

He'd never find Lily if she were unconscious.

Fortifying his heart for the worst-case scenario, he stomped the fiery floor past the kitchen where the blaze raged.

She wasn't in her room.

Nor his.

He checked the bathroom.

"Nick!

Thank God! His knees felt weak while his spirit lifted. He closed the door to keep the flames out, then tore off the mask and crushed her in a desperate hug. She was wet and shivering under his flannel shirt. "Are you okay?"

"Yes!"

"I gotta get you outta here right now!"

"The window's boarded from the outside."

"I know." Nick took aim with the axe. "It's

gonna be a tight squeeze, but I think you'll fit."

"No! I'm going with you."

"No way."

"I need you, Nick. We go together, or I'm not going at all."

There was no use wasting time arguing. "Okay, okay." Trapped, with no choice except to fight the fire on the other side of the door, he kissed her one more time. "Ready?"

She nodded, not knowing the hell she was about to go through.

"Wait!" She pressed her palms to his chest. "Nick, I didn't take the pill. I could never do that. I got my period the next day. But I swear I didn't take it."

Confused and relieved by her untimely admission, he said, "Well, if we're making confessions, I bought your house. I was gonna give it to you for Christmas." Then he covered her head to toe with the blanket, tossed her body over his shoulder like a sack of sugar, and went back into the fire.

Blinded by thick smoke, he couldn't pass the flames spewing from the kitchen. He held Lily tight, praying the water truck would douse the house any moment.

There was a terrifying crack over the din, then the frighteningly familiar shake, rattle, and roar of the walls coming down.

Chapter Twenty

"Wha…happ…?" Lily's raw throat produced nothing but a painful whisper as she lie on a gurney in the hospital. She may not have remembered fainting the last time she was here, but this time she had a clear memory of the events that brought her to this place. Again.

What could have started the fire? Ancient electrical wiring? The hot oven? The candle and the curtain?

More importantly—*what happened to Nick?*

She clawed at the tubes in her nostrils until the nurse anchored her arm to the mattress, while the other arm was already strapped to her chest.

"Take it easy. You're going to be just fine," the nurse said.

"What happened?" By the time she found her voice, it was too late. The nurse slipped a sedative into the catheter line taped to her hand. The overhead florescent lights flickered a few times before everything faded to black.

When she woke again, she was alone in a dim room, listening to the low beeps from the monitor beside her bed.

Lily didn't need anyone to tell her the house had burned down. She smelled the char in her hair. Felt the sticky grime on her skin. Tasted the smoke every time she coughed.

If it wasn't for Nick...

So, where was he now? That was all she wanted to know.

Please, God, let him be okay. Let. Him. Be. Okay. Please. God.

As the meds wore off, panic rushed in, making Lily's heart race. The nurse dosed her again without explanation, and she fell back into a comfortably numb sleep without a care in the world, with Nick's name as the last word on her lips.

****

Nick stood beside Lily as she slept peacefully in the hospital bed. White gauze covered the lacerations on her forehead. She'd survive the broken arm and second-degree burns on her lower legs and feet. Minor injuries that could have been so much worse.

Miraculously, he'd escaped without a scrape, just the wind knocked out of him from some falling sheetrock.

She suffered the brunt of the damage after he dropped her, then landed on top of her, protecting and injuring her at the same time.

Her house was old, but the solid framework held up better than he'd expected. *Thank God.*

The girl got lucky.

So did he.

He stroked her cheek with the back of his fingers, and her eyes fluttered opened.

"Santa?" she mumbled.

He'd slipped back into the red jacket since he had no spare clothes in his truck. "Lily, it's me,

Nick." Careful of the catheter line, he took her hand and kissed it. "How do you feel?"

"I'm fine...now that you're here. I was so worried about you." The monitor registered her rising heartbeat.

"You need to rest. They wanna keep you here a few days for observation. You inhaled some smoke. Got a few burns. But other than that we're okay."

"I'm so sorry. I didn't mean to be so much trouble."

"What are you talking about? You're no trouble at all."

She rolled her eyes. "Nick, I burned down the house."

"Don't worry about it. Just concentrate on getting better."

"I feel better already with you here." A tear rolled down her smudged cheek and he caught it with his fingertip.

"I know exactly how you feel." He plucked a tissue from the box and dabbed her eyes.

"I need to tell you something..."

"You can tell me tomorrow."

"No, I have to tell you now. I just want to say...I love you. I was afraid to admit it before, but I'm not afraid any more. I want you to know that. Because I'd regret never telling you how I feel."

Maybe her words were a side effect from the drugs in her I.V. drip but he'd take them just the same. "That's what I've been telling you all this time. But you didn't believe me."

The nurse came in, breaking up their conversation, and hustled him out the door. "Time for Mr. Claus to get back to the North Pole. It's sleepy time for Mrs. Claus. He can visit again tomorrow."

****

The next day, Lily felt a little better. It was Christmas Eve, and Nick was here.

He surfed the channels on the tiny television mounted on the wall and found an old time classic, "March of the Wooden Soldiers." She hadn't watched it since she was a little girl. It was the scene where the Crooked Old Man makes a claim for Little Bo Peep's hand in marriage, and in exchange, he'd tear up Old Mother Hubbard's mortgage.

She couldn't thank Nick enough for lifting her out of her financial hole, although all that was left of her home was a big hole in the ground. But that was a discussion for another time.

"All I want for Christmas now is shower and a pair of pajamas." Her gauze-wrapped hair reeked of stale smoke, and the mint-green hospital gown revealed more than it concealed.

"The doctor said to wait another day. How's your appetite?"

"I can eat. What's on the menu tonight?" She studied the piece of paper on her bedside table.

"Not hospital food, that's for sure." From behind the curtain, Nick rolled a cart with a cardboard box on top. "I know it's not a traditional Christmas feast, but I figured a burger from the diner would be the next best thing. And some spring rolls from Zhang's Chinese take-out."

"How did you know about the spring rolls?" Maybe he was a mind reader after all.

"You mentioned it once."

"Wow." His attention to detail was impressive.

He cut her food so she could eat it with her one good hand. Then he popped the cork on a bottle.

"Champagne? In a hospital?"

"Non-alcoholic sparkling cider." He flashed the label before filling two clear plastic cups. "Peach."

"Yum."

Then he set a small decorative tree on a spare table.

Her heart swelled at his thoughtfulness. "Gosh, I feel so special."

"As you should."

"You didn't have to go through all this trouble."

"What trouble?"

"The food. The cider. *And* a tree."

"This is no trouble at all. You have to admit, it feels a lot more like Christmas, dontcha think?"

She nodded. He was right. The holiday bonsai tree was the perfect touch. "I'm just happy you came back to see me."

"Lily, I wanna spend Christmas with you no matter where you are."

At the end of visiting hours, the nurse came in to kick him out for the night.

"Merry Christmas, sugar." He dropped a kiss on her lips. "I hope Santa brings you everything you want."

Although she wished he could stay longer, she didn't want to be greedy with all he'd given her, so she simply smiled. "He already did."

****

Lily drifted off to sleep sometime before

midnight and woke when the nurse made a final check of her vitals before the change of the guards.

After a few minutes of lying there, staring at the dark ceiling, the door opened again and someone entered. She recognized the red suit as anyone would.

"Hi, Santa," she whispered.

Nick pulled off the hat, revealing his own dark locks, then yanked down the beard. He shut the door behind him and flicked on the soft light in the corner of the room.

"Ho-ho-ho," he said in a low voice. He leaned over the bed rail and kissed her with his delicious cinnamon-flavored lips.

"You're really getting some miles outta that costume, huh?"

"What do ya mean?" He smiled. "I'm just doing my job."

"What happened to your belly, Santa?" Lily pressed the button that angled the bed so she could sit upright, getting a better look at him.

"Yeah, well..." He patted the red and white fur hanging loose around his middle. "What can I say? Santa's been working out."

"You know it's too late for visitors. They'll kick you out when they catch you in here."

"Not this time. I'm not going anywhere tonight. The chief gave me an all-access pass for Christmas."

"I'll have to thank him."

"By the way..." He reached into his pocket and pulled out a slip of paper, wrinkled yet recognizable. "He also gave me this. He thought Santa might know where to find an *emotionally available* man for a special young woman."

She couldn't control the stupid smile filling her face, no matter how hard she tried. "Um, what are you talking about?"

"Oh, so this doesn't ring a bell?" He flipped the paper over, showing her both sides before handing it to her. "Maybe it's from someone else from Barbieri's Barbershop. Maybe Bob. Or Sophia."

Her cheeks got hot. Caught asking for a man for Christmas was as desperate as it gets. "Well, maybe it's mine. I mean, it could be mine. I don't remember. An *emotionally available* man is quite a request for Santa to fill."

"You're telling me. But I think I can handle it." He gave her a sideways glance. "Are you sure you can handle me?"

"God, I'm so embarrassed."

"Don't be. I just wanted to make sure you were okay with your Christmas gift." He waved his hands down his body. "Considering what you did to the *other* gift..."

Hiding her face in her hand, she groaned, "Please don't remind me."

"We'll talk about rebuilding once you're outta here. In the meantime, as long as this emotionally available man is okay by you, I have something else..." He didn't wait for her response. Just pulled out a red velvet box and flipped open the lid.

"Nick, really...I don't need anything. All I want for Christmas is you." Breathless at the revelation of the glittering diamond inside, the pear-shaped stone set high in the simple gold setting looked just like the ring her mother had worn before hocking her valuables to pay the bills. "Where did you get this?"

"The Swap 'N Shop." His eyes twinkled.

"But *how* did you know?"

"Know what—that it was your mother's? I didn't. But the man who sold it to me did. I took a chance and looked into buying back Britney's ring— the one she accused you of stealing—hoping she'd leave you alone. I didn't know Mark's full name so I mentioned yours. The owner said he knew you. He had this in the vault with your name on it. He'd been holding onto it all these years because he didn't have the heart to sell it, in case you ever came looking for it."

"I didn't even know about it."

"Well, it's all here." He put a small shoebox on her tray.

"All?" Joyful tears stung the backs of her eyes as she looked inside and found all the precious things she'd thought were long gone. "I-I don't know what to say."

"Just say thank you."

She shook her head. "Thanking you isn't enough."

"Then spend your life with me and we'll call it even."

A nervous giggle escaped in response to his informal proposal, afraid to say anything in case it was his idea of an early April Fool's prank.

"So, even when I'm standing here, fulfilling your letter to Santa in the flesh, you still doubt me?" Shaking his head disappointedly, he pulled out another little box and opened it.

Lily was breathless. "Oh, Nick. Is this for me?"

"Of course, it's for you. Only this one didn't come from the Swap 'n Shop. It's brand new, never been worn, no history, no baggage, no nothing. But I can hold onto it for you until you're ready to wear it."

She took the box from his fingers to get a closer look. The center diamond was bigger than a sugarcoated peanut from Brawny's Fall Festival. Now she really didn't know what to say.

"If you don't like it, you can always exchange it for something else, like a new car."

Lily cut her eyes at him. "Don't be ridiculous. It's beautiful."

"No. *You're* beautiful. That's just a ring."

"Oh, Nick. I love it."

He exhaled. "God, you have no idea how relieved I am to hear you say that. I was worried that you might throw it at me, then throw me outta here permanently."

"I told you..." She dabbed her tears with a tissue. "I'm not afraid any more. I love you and that's that."

"You're sure you like it?"

"I do," she cooed, never so pleasantly surprised. "I absolutely, positively do." She studied the diamond clusters through misty eyes. "Wait—is it an engagement ring or a..."

"Wedding ring?" A distinct blush crept upon his face that she hadn't witnessed until now. "I just took a chance and bought both. In case you say yes. I don't mind a long engagement if that'll make you happy. Get to know each other better first like you said. But I saw the rings together and thought you'd like 'em."

She handed him the box.

Nick's face fell. "What's the matter?"

"Nothing."

"Then, why are you giving it back?"

"So, you can put it on my finger, silly Santa."

His smile stretched slowly. "Oh. Okay. In that case..." He got down on one knee. "Lily Lane, will you do me the honor of becoming my wife?"

Her heart fluttered in bliss like she'd never felt before, making the machine blip wildly. "Yes, Nicholas Knight. There's nothing in the world I want more."

He plucked the ring from the cushion, slipped it on her finger, and pressed his lips to her hand, sealing his proposal with a kiss.

"But after everything you gave me for Christmas, I have nothing to give you." Then a big idea crossed her mind. "Well, maybe there's one thing..."

He stared at her curiously confused. "What do you mean?"

She waggled her eyebrows at his baggy red pants and licked her lips. "Maybe I can, um, you know...kiss your candy cane?"

Nick laughed so hard he was nearly ho-ho-ho-ing. "Well, now look what you've done. You got Santa all ho-ho-hot and bothered. I like the way you think, but I say we save it for the ho-ho-honeymoon, Mrs. Claus. Or at least until you're outta the ho-ho-hospital."

Epilogue

One year later

Nick paced the hospital floor in a glorious haze, with a dumbstruck smile plastered to his face, more amped up than a kid on Christmas morning. He hadn't felt this incredible since Valentine's Day, standing beside Lily at the altar in town hall.

For a guy with next to no sleep for the past forty-eight hours, he was functioning fairly well.

As tired as he was, he couldn't stop staring through the maternity ward window at the special delivery in the incubator marked with his last name.

On his second Christmas with Lily, they were blessed with the greatest gift she could ever give him—offspring.

Twins in fact.

A boy and a girl. A little early. But healthy, which was all that mattered.

The double dose of adorableness made his heart flutter every time he looked at them, still finding it hard to believe they were his. Theirs.

Born ten minutes to midnight on Christmas Eve, their son came first. They named him Nicholas after the proud papa, of course.

Shortly thereafter, in the wee hours of Christmas

Morning, their daughter made her grand entrance. They called her Natalie for two reasons—she was born on Christmas Day and it had been Lily's mother's name.

As if the holidays weren't hectic enough, they were in the process of rebuilding the house that had burnt to the ground. A new construction on the land that had once belonged to Lily's parents made their home sweet home even more bittersweet and sentimental. She didn't argue when he suggested they live in his camper until their house was ready. It might be a tight squeeze for a little while, but he could never be close enough when it came to her.

Funny how things worked out. For once, everything was perfect. His life. His babies. His marriage. But life was crazy like that sometimes. All of a sudden, before you know it, you're living happily ever after.

A word about the author...

Debra is thrilled to be working with The Wild Rose Press on her first published novel—a sensual contemporary Christmas romance entitled *Sleeping With Santa.*

Meshing her love of Christmastime-anytime with her appetite for steamy romances into one passionate package, she hopes you enjoy reading *Sleeping With Santa* as much as she enjoyed writing it.

Up next on her to-do list is drafting two more sensual Christmas romances, also set on Long Island, in the fictitious harbor town of Scenic View, New York.

You can find out more about Debra on her website at:

www.DebraDruzy.com.

WITHDRAWN

Made in the USA
Middletown, DE
02 December 2014